The
SIGN
PAINTER

Center Point
Large Print

Also by Davis Bunn and available from
Center Point Large Print:

Lion of Babylon
Book of Dreams
Rare Earth
Hidden in Dreams
Strait of Hormuz
Unlimited

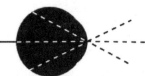

**This Large Print Book carries the
Seal of Approval of N.A.V.H.**

The SIGN PAINTER

Davis Bunn

CENTER POINT LARGE PRINT
THORNDIKE, MAINE

This Center Point Large Print edition is published
in the year 2014 by arrangement with Howard Books,
a division of Simon & Schuster, Inc.

Copyright © 2014 by T. Davis Bunn.

The text of this Large Print edition is unabridged.
In other aspects, this book may vary from the original edition.
Printed in the United States of America on permanent paper.
Set in 16-point Times New Roman type.

ISBN: 978-1-62899-217-5

Library of Congress Cataloging-in-Publication Data

Bunn, T. Davis, 1952–
The Sign painter / Davis Bunn. — Center Point Large Print edition.
pages ; cm
Summary: "A young mother struggles to get back on her feet after a
devastating loss leaves her and her daughter alone and living on the
street"—Provided by publisher.
ISBN 978-1-62899-217-5 (library bindng : alk. paper)
1. Sign painting—Fiction. 2. Large type books. I. Title.
PS3552.U4718S55 2014b
813'.54—dc23
2014019467

This book is dedicated
to all those who help rebuild
lives and hearts and homes,
one miracle at a time.

Home is where the heart is.
—PLINY THE ELDER
ROME, FIRST CENTURY

— Chapter 1 —

Amy Dowell considered herself a very good mother. She did not allow her circumstances to dictate how much love she had to give. She did not permit the presence of worries to color the way she greeted her daughter. "Good morning, darling."

"I don't want to get up."

"I know, sweetheart."

"It got loud last night."

"But we were safe here inside our little home, weren't we?"

"In our love cave."

"That's right. Here, let me slip this over your head."

"Can't I sleep a little while more, Mommy?"

"No, Kimmie, we have to get a move on."

"But why? I'm so sleepy."

"Because I have a new job this morning. I told you last night, remember? Kimmie, let go of your pillow, honey. Give me your foot. Now the other one. Okay, here we go, ready to face the world?"

A delivery truck chose that very moment to start up. Amy's daughter had hated the sound of truck engines ever since the two of them had been forced onto the road. It was why they seldom

9

stayed in truck stops. The rumbling motors gave her terrible nightmares.

Kimmie scrunched herself into the crook of her mother's neck and squealed. Amy raised her voice to be heard over the departing truck. "It's all right, honey. It's leaving."

"The big bad truck wants to eat me!"

"No, it doesn't, darling. There, see, it's gone now." Amy dropped the plastic holdall with their washing items into her backpack. She had a purse, but it remained stowed in the cabinet over the sink. Carrying a purse was something from a different life. Amy waited until the truck had merged with the sparse dawn traffic to open the door. By mid-May, central Florida was already hot and sticky at six-thirty in the morning. Kimmie was big enough to walk under her own steam, but Amy carried her anyway. It was hard managing the flimsy stairs while hefting her daughter and the bulky pack. But she had grown used to much harder tasks than this one.

Their home was a camper cab bolted to a Ford truck. The pickup had a hundred and seventy-two thousand hard miles, and the massive eight-cylinder motor sucked gas. The tires were bald and the front windshield was cracked. The previous evening, Amy had parked in a service station's rear lot, behind the car wash. After the nine p.m. shift change, the lone attendant of such stations rarely left the bulletproof enclosure.

A year back, Amy never would have dreamed that such knowledge might prove vital. Or that she would become proficient at picking locks, which she managed with Kimmie wrapped around her neck. All service stations had cameras surveying the restroom doors. But at six-thirty in the morning, half an hour before the shift ended, the attendant rarely paid attention to the security screens. Amy opened the restroom lock in ten seconds flat.

Once they were cleaned up, Amy returned to the camper and gave careful attention to Kimmie's hair. The five-year-old whined a bit over the inevitable tangles but mostly stayed quiet. By now Kimberly was familiar with their new-city routine. So much depended upon them both putting on their best face. Kimberly had hair like summer wheat, dry and blond and so fine that it poofed out with static electricity when brushed hard. Sometimes that was good for a laugh, but not this morning. Amy was in a hurry, and Kimmie was still sleepy.

Amy dressed her daughter in a clean T-shirt and jeans, then let Kimmie curl up with her blanket in the passenger seat. Amy flattened the sheet of instructions she had copied down the previous evening from MapQuest. Another thing she had mastered over the past eighteen months was finding her way through strange cities.

As they turned onto Highway 192, Brentonville's main thoroughfare, a pair of police cars came flashing past. Amy could not completely hide her flinch. Her fear of cops was genuine and well founded. Her most dread nightmare was of some new city's social services trying to steal Kimmie away. Not to mention the fact that her vehicle was a rolling list of violations. No one knew cops like the homeless. It was a fact of life on the road.

The church was easy enough to locate. The main building rose north of the thoroughfare that ran arrow-straight to Disney. It was good that Kimmie was drowsing, because they passed a giant sign advertising the theme parks farther west. That was all Amy needed, having her daughter freak out over how close they were to the Magic Kingdom.

The First Methodist Church complex dominated two full city blocks. Amy had researched it on her laptop the previous day, after the job offer had been confirmed. Most big cities had at least one such church, where the problems of today's world were not hidden beyond the barrier of faith. There were websites dedicated to people like Amy, live boards that posted helpful information about every city in the nation. Some of the sites were specifically designed to help single mothers: where to go, where to stay, what to avoid. How to survive.

Newcomers without roots were not always welcome in churches. Which was why Amy parked her truck at the back of the church lot, then brushed Kimmie's hair a second time and fitted in the two pink plastic hair clips and straightened her T-shirt before getting in close to her daughter and saying, "What are we going to do when we get inside?"

"Smile and be nice," Kimmie replied.

"That's my good girl."

"Will they have eggs, Mommy?"

She took the little girl's hand. "Why don't we go and see?"

Many city churches with schools and day-care centers served breakfast for students and families. These days, too many of their charges arrived hungry. This free meal was generally restricted to people signed into the system. Others had to pay. Sometimes, though, Amy was able to slip in. It just depended on the church and the day. As they joined the line, she saw a father with three young boys set money on the counter. Amy gave a silent sigh and reached into her jeans. She hated having to use her gas money for food, but she needed a safe place to leave Kimmie.

The desk inside the cafeteria doors was staffed by a woman with an expression that Amy had come to know all too well. The woman's name tag read LUCY. Her no-nonsense gaze held the hard-earned wisdom of having long experience with Amy's world.

"You're new," the woman said.

"We just arrived last night." Amy tried to make her voice as cheery as possible.

Lucy motioned for Amy to swing around to the side of the desk. The woman continued to accept breakfast vouchers as she asked, "Where from?"

Amy knew the administrator's easy tone masked a well-honed ability to sense trouble before it started. The only way to handle a person like this was not to try and handle her. People like Lucy had heard all the hard-luck pleas and were not moved. Amy gave it to her honest and straight. "Tampa, and before that, Tallahassee. Before that, Atlanta."

Kimmie reached for her mother's hand and said softly, "I didn't like 'Lanta."

"Neither of us did," Amy agreed.

The woman smiled a greeting to a young family and asked, "So why go?"

"Work. I was a graphic designer, you know . . ."

"Before," the woman supplied, looking at her with a glint of what might have been sympathy. "And now?"

"Mommy paints pretty windows," Kimmie said, a trace of genuine pride in her voice.

"I'm a sign painter," Amy explained.

The woman appeared won over by Kimmie. "You have work?"

"Supposedly. At Denton Chevrolet. I won't know for sure until I show up."

"And you need a place for your little one to stay." She smiled as she handed Amy two breakfast vouchers. "Go eat. I'll stop by later. We'll chat."

Amy fumbled her thanks and hated how her fingers trembled as she stuffed the crumpled bills back in her jeans. The woman noticed. Amy suspected that Lucy missed very little. She gave Amy another smile, one survivor to another, and said to Kimmie, "I believe I saw them making waffles."

Kimmie's delight was genuine. "My favorite!"

Amy thanked the woman again and joined the breakfast line. She gave her eyes a quick swipe when she thought no one was watching. She had grown used to this, how an unexpected kindness threatened to unravel her control.

Amy filled Kimmie's plate with sausage and waffles, then took eggs and sausage and hash browns and biscuits for herself. Kimberly hated how the syrup ran over her sausage, but the little girl had learned not to say anything. They walked down the central aisle. Amy veered away from the first table with free seats because of the man she spotted just as she was about to sit down. He was in his late forties, and very handsome in a chiseled fashion, and clearly a cop. Which was why the only other people seated at the table with him were church workers. The man might as well have had a stone wall built around him. No one else even looked his way. Amy was far from the only person in the room harboring bad memories from run-ins with the police.

Amy spotted two places at a table holding several Bibles. She smiled a greeting and let Kimmie snuggle up next to her on the bench. The room was filled with pinched features and faces bearing the remnants of a leathery tan. Many of the gazes were hooded and fiercely aware, all products of life on the street. Amy knew she was gaining some of the same tell-tales and was helpless to do anything about it. Another of her nightmares was waking up one morning and discovering the same traits drawn on Kimberly's young face.

There was no conversation at their table. This was another thing she once found remarkable and now accepted as normal, how silent most people were. People on the verge knew others had no interest in hearing their worries. They also knew someone here might be very close to exploding and could be set off by the smallest word. Quiet was safe.

Lucy took a seat at the table across the aisle and watched as Amy helped Kimmie cut her waffle and sausage. When Amy finished her meal, she unzipped her pack and pulled out a Bible. The woman observed that, too. Amy had no idea why Lucy was so interested in them. But eighteen months on the road had taught her to judge people swiftly and well. She sensed no danger from Lucy. Amy opened her Bible to the passage that was listed on the board by the front podium. Let the woman watch.

The woman stepped to the front podium and introduced herself as Lucy Watts, head of the church's outreach ministries. She led them in prayer, then preached a brief sermon. Amy followed the words with determined intensity. These daily lessons were a vital part of her holding on to what was most precious in her life, including the ability to set aside all her worries and burdens, and show her young daughter the love she needed. Amy had learned to clamp down on the questions for which there were no answers. Such as how God could allow these things to happen, or when they would find a way out of their impossible situation, or where she could offer her daughter a future. Stability. A home. All the things that had become impossible dreams. All the things that Amy was determined to regain.

When Lucy left the podium, she walked down the aisle, greeting several latecomers and hugging one woman who rose from Amy's table. Lucy seated herself across the table from Amy. She reached over and swung Amy's Bible around. The two pages were underlined, with thoughts and prayers written into the margins. "A student of the Word. I like that."

"It's all that holds my life together."

"I know what you mean." Lucy's gaze drifted over the rapidly emptying room. "I wish I could wake up a few of the nodders to that same truth."

"I can't condemn them," Amy replied. "I'd probably have given in to the same bitterness, except for one thing."

Lucy watched Amy stroke her daughter's hair. "Where do you live?"

"My husband's camper. It was actually his dad's. He used it for hunting trips." Amy looked down at her little one. "I was after him for years to get rid of that old thing."

"You lost him?"

"Twenty-two months ago." The terse response was all that was required. Amy settled her hand over her daughter's ear and pressed so that the other ear was covered by her body. "Cancer."

"You lost your home?"

"No. First I lost my job. Then my health benefits. Then I declared bankruptcy. The home went last."

Kimmie squirmed and pushed Amy's hand away. "I can't breathe, Mommy."

"Sorry, darling."

Lucy rose from her place. "Mind showing me where you live?"

The Ford pickup had never looked more battered. The camper's rust spots were glaring blemishes in the morning sun. The door shuddered as Amy pulled it open. The old vehicle seemed as embarrassed as she was over having someone see how they lived. Amy had forgotten how loudly the right rear suspension creaked when someone climbed the stairs. Lucy entered and slipped into one of the two chairs by the narrow fold-down table. She gave the cabin a very slow look.

Amy settled on the bed and pulled Kimmie into her lap. She had no idea why Lucy was here. But she knew an interview when she saw one. For what, Amy had no idea. Even so, she felt a faint thrill of electricity run up her spine. Maybe, just maybe, this woman would give Kimmie a free place in their day-care center. It would make all the difference in the world, knowing her little girl was taken care of by people like Lucy while Amy was off at work. Making money. Trying to climb out of this hole.

Lucy pointed at the drawings taped over the window above the sink. "Your daughter has real talent."

"Did you hear that, honey? The nice lady likes your art."

"Mommy only puts up the ones that make her happy."

"What's your name, sweetheart?"

"Kimmie."

"How old are you?"

"Almost five and a half."

Amy added, "In two months."

19

"That's 'almost,' isn't it, Mommy?"

"Yes, darling. You're my big good girl."

Lucy asked, "You select the drawings that are happy?"

"It's the best reinforcement I can give her," Amy replied. She heard the shiver in her own voice. *Please, oh, please let this woman give my baby a day-care place and for free!*

Lucy nodded and did not speak. She continued to look around the cramped confines. Amy's gaze tracked along with hers. She saw the battered equipment and the neat rows of possessions, the shelf with Kimmie's toys and dolls, the shelf where their clothes were folded, the scruffy cabinet with the cans of emergency food and their two plates and two cups and two knives and forks. The narrow sink beneath the opposite window was clean; the drying rack held their soup bowls and glasses and spoons from dinner the previous night.

Finally, Lucy rose from her chair and started for the door. "Come with me."

Together they walked through the parking lot shared by the outreach center and a small medical clinic and the crisis pregnancy center. Lucy took them along a covered walk past the main church buildings, crossed a street, and stood before what formerly was a down-at-the-heels strip motel. Amy's heart started beating so fast, she thought it might escape from her chest.

"The church acquired this property two years ago. Volunteers converted it into nineteen studio apartments."

Kimmie protested, "Mommy, you're squeezing my hand!"

Amy swept her daughter up into her arms. She did not trust herself to speak.

Lucy fished a key from her pocket and unlocked a door. "The family in here until the day before yesterday has been moved into a home built by Habitat for Humanity. Normally, I only give our apartments to church members, or families recommended by a local relief group. But just before you showed up this morning, I felt God whisper to me."

The studio apartment was freshly painted and had a kitchenette and a real dining table. There was a door with a lock and pale curtains and a foldout sofa and a sleeping pallet rolled up in the corner. There was a bathroom. With hot water. And a shower.

It was a palace.

Kimmie whispered, "Mommy, is this for us?"

Amy could only nod.

"Let me down! Let me down!"

Amy allowed her squirming daughter to slip from her arms. She had no choice. Her strength was gone. She could scarcely hold herself erect. She felt tears course down her face.

Lucy had clearly seen it all before. "Why don't

I leave you folks to settle in. You can come by later and we'll go through the forms."

Amy managed, "I need to go see about this new job."

"So call me when you get back."

"I have no idea when that will be." Amy heard her voice break over the words and did not care. "All these jobs are rush-rush."

"Girl, believe me, I don't serve with this ministry so I can work from nine to five. Your daughter is welcome in our day care. We run a special after-hours service for working moms." The outreach director set the key on the table by the sofa. "Welcome home."

When the door shut, Amy did not so much fall to her knees as feel the carpet rise up to meet her. Kimmie was suddenly in her arms. The little one was crying, too. Her daughter's joy was as great as her own.

This was another lesson the road had taught them both. How much it could hurt to hope again.

— Chapter 2 —

Paul Travers waited in Lucy Watts's office, surrounded by the din of a vibrant church community. Two walls were glass from the waist up, granting Paul a clear view of a social room with a massive sound system, and a study room filled with computer gear and a wall of books. The books looked well worn, and the computer terminals were decorated with so many stickers that it was hard to see their original color. Paul figured the outreach director was an expert at riding herd over teens.

When Lucy Watts walked into the office, Granville Burnes, the man who had asked Paul down for this meeting, asked, "You gave them the place?"

"I did. Yes."

"The board is gonna ask you some hard questions."

"It will be a pleasure, dealing with the board."

Granville was a former detective who now ran the church's security program. His voice was a comfortable growl. "So it was like you said. A miracle."

"Before my first cup of coffee." Lucy turned his way. "Paul Travers, did I get your name right? Come on in. Granville, why don't you join us?"

Lucy and Granville both carried the hard-edged wisdom of the street. They gave Paul a penetrating inspection as he settled into the chair opposite Lucy's desk. The director's walls were decorated with degrees in counseling and ministerial studies. There were pictures of her sharing big grins with various people, breaking ground on the building where they sat, Lucy accepting some award, and her standing with families before different houses.

"My power wall," Lucy said, following his gaze. "All of the people you see there are miracles in the making. People who have come back from nothing and made genuine successes of their lives and their families. Helps remind me of what we're doing here."

"It's a beautiful sight," Paul agreed. "And important on the bad days."

She leaned back in her chair. "What do you know about bad days, Mr. Travers?"

"Call me Paul. I know a little."

"You ever been homeless, Paul?"

"No."

"Ever gone hungry?"

"Yes, but not how you mean. Never from need."

Lucy was big-boned and strong and handsome. And she did not like him. Paul assumed she had a thing about cops. Many people with street experience could smell a cop at fifty paces. For

24

them, the fact that Paul worked exclusively for churches and religious organizations did not mean a thing. Lucy asked, "Why are you here?"

"My pastor said you had a problem. I came."

"Paul's pastor and I have been prayer partners for years," Granville offered. "He and I share a lot of secrets."

Lucy's gaze remained iron-hard. "Did Granville tell you what our problem was?"

"No."

"But you came anyway. Just dropped everything and flew down from Baltimore."

"Actually, I drove." Paul knew she was probing and did not mind. "I do this a lot."

"Do what, exactly? Sorry, Granville hasn't told me much about you. When I asked, he said he wanted me to meet you first. Which, you've got to understand, is not exactly the sort of answer that would reassure me."

"I was a federal agent for nine years. First at headquarters in Washington, then at our Baltimore field office."

"Why did you quit?"

"Four years ago, I was injured while on active duty. I was given a medical discharge. While I was getting back on my feet, I got a call from my pastor. He told me about a problem a religious organization was having."

"What kind of problem?"

"Sorry. I can't say. Just like I'll never talk

25

about yours. If I can help." Paul gave an easy shrug. "I've basically been troubleshooting ever since. You can call it my personal ministry, if that makes you any more comfortable."

Lucy drilled him with a gaze, dark and tense. "You a believer, Paul Travers?"

"I am. Yes."

"You recognize the passage I spoke about this morning?"

"Sure. The Samaritan woman who met Jesus at the well. You gave a great talk."

"You have any further thoughts about that particular passage?"

Paul liked how she tied this to faith. Clearly, the church was experiencing a problem, something that troubled these two very much. Something big enough and dark enough that they did not want to take it to their elders. Paul guessed they feared going to the local authorities. If they did, some church leaders might use it to threaten the outreach center's very existence. He had known such situations before. There were always congregation members who disliked any activity that was not directly tied to the regular services. So Lucy and Granville were sitting here, alone and vulnerable, desperate for someone they could trust with their secret. And what they wanted to know most of all was did he share their need for Jesus. He did not know them, but he liked them both. A lot.

Paul replied, "I've always liked how this outcast woman became his first real missionary. The fourth chapter of John, verses thirty-nine through forty-two, describes how she tells other Samaritans about her meeting with Jesus. Her own personal transformation and testimony are so powerful that many of the Samaritans believe even before they meet with Jesus. They go out and find him because of her. Jesus stays with them for two days and brings even more of them to faith. All of this within the community of outcasts."

Lucy glanced at the burly man seated next to Paul, then said, "To answer your question, Paul, we have a problem. A huge one."

"We don't have enough evidence to prove anything," Granville added. "But it's real."

Paul nodded, glad he had made the trip. "How can I help?"

— Chapter 3 —

Amy left Kimmie in the church's day-care center and drove slowly past the front of the car dealership. She did not stop. She had no intention of letting anyone there see her ride. To do so would reveal how desperate she was for this work. Especially now, when there was a chance to give Kimmie a real home again.

But she wouldn't think about that now. She had been forced to pull over and cry twice on the way from the church. The joy would sweep over her in sudden waves. Amy took a hard breath and said to the sunlight on her windshield, "Get a grip, girl."

She found a parking space on the road behind the dealership. She cut the motor and slipped back into the camper. She brushed her hair, a few shades darker than Kimberly's, more coppery than blond, with some distinct red highlights. She fitted a leather-knit belt over the starched white short-sleeved shirt and cinched it tight. Her lace-up boots were badly worn, but her jeans were long enough to hide most of the scars. Amy climbed up on the little plastic stool and pulled her second backpack, the one with her art tools, from the top cabinet. She opened the zipper and did a quick check to ensure that she had all she needed. Then she gave her reflection a hard look and repeated what she had said to her daughter that morning. "What are we going to do when we get inside?" She gave the mirror her brightest look and exclaimed happily, "Smile and be nice!"

She climbed down to the street, locked her camper, and started along the sidewalk. What she had seen in her reflection dogged her every step. But there was nothing she could do about the jagged edges in her gaze.

• • •

Bob Denton, owner of Denton Chevrolet, was a man made to smile. Only he wasn't smiling now. He was gaping. At her.

Amy knew she was still attractive. Her beauty had once been a source of confidence. Nowadays, more often than not, it made her feel vulnerable. But Bob Denton did not threaten. He simply stared.

Denton had the ruddy cheerfulness of a good old boy and spoke with a distinct Florida twang. Amy's father had been born and raised in Perry, a small town in the center of the state, about halfway between Jacksonville and Tallahassee. Both of Amy's parents had been only children, and the grandparents were long gone. Bob Denton sounded a lot like the kin she no longer had.

Bob asked, "Where are you from?"

"My husband and I called Alexandria home. That ended two years ago."

"And now?"

"Basically, I go where the work takes me. I hope to be staying here."

He asked, "In Orlando?"

"Brentonville, more like. We've made some church friends. We feel welcome."

"You and your husband?"

"No, my husband passed away two years ago. Now it's just me and my little girl."

She could see his Adam's apple working and

knew he was nervous. Which, oddly, left her feeling calm. He said, "I'm sorry for your loss."

"Mr. Denton, could we talk about the work you have for me?"

"Oh, right, sure thing. I, ah . . ." He opened a file and pulled out some sketches, all without taking his eyes off her. "These are just some rough ideas."

It was pretty much as she expected. The company was getting rid of excess inventory with a blowout sale. They wanted this message emblazoned on their windows. "Sure, I can do this, no problem." Amy flipped through the pages, basically to give her something to do other than return his stare. "I did pretty much the same kind of display for Vickers Cadillac in Tampa. You know Mr. Vickers; I believe he called you."

"That's right, he did." His swallow was audible. "Which church?"

"I'm sorry?"

"Where your friends are. In Brentonville."

"First Methodist."

His eyes grew round. "That's where I go."

She dropped her gaze back to the sheets. "When do you need this work done by?"

"The sale starts Sunday, day after tomorrow."

"That's tight, but I can do it. I'll need to work at night. Can you please make sure your security people are aware that I'll be working outside of normal hours?"

"Sure. I mean, you'll be here all night?"

"To get this done on time, I'll need to work more or less around the clock. Tonight I'll leave and get my little girl fed and settled, then I can come back and . . ." She hesitated, then decided there was no reason not to say, "Mr. Denton, isn't this the point when you ask me about my price?"

He jerked back. "I'm sorry. It's just . . . How much?"

Normally, this was when Amy's desperation showed. But today was different. Maybe it was how the man kept staring; maybe it was the miracle she had just experienced at the church. Whatever the reason, she stayed calm enough to take the price she had come in with and double it. "Twelve hundred dollars for the rush job. Like I said, to get this done on time, I'll be working flat out from now until Saturday morning."

He did not even blink. "Fine."

"I'll need half now, please."

He scribbled on a form and handed it across his desk. "Give this to my assistant."

"Great." Her smile was genuine. "Thank you, Mr. Denton. You'll be getting my very best work."

He rose with her, which had not happened in so long that Amy felt uncomfortable with Bob Denton's manners. She felt his gaze on her as she started for the door. "Ms. Dowell."

"Yes?"

He swallowed again. "Nothing. Thank you for coming in. You've made my day."

For twelve hundred dollars, the man deserved the truth. "That makes two of us, Mr. Denton. Really."

— Chapter 4 —

At three that afternoon, Paul was parked in a car four blocks from the church. The street was typical for many tourist towns, a seedy afterthought that remained well hidden from the hordes taking aim for the shiny delights at the end of the money rainbow.

The four-door Mercury's front seat was as comfortable as a sofa on a lazy Sunday. Granville Burnes, the retired Brentonville detective, sat behind the wheel. The car's color was faded and unimportant. Paul's door had two rust measles, but the shocks were reinforced and the massive engine was in top form. Granville asked, "You ever sat stakeout before, Travers?"

"Many times."

"Yeah? Where was that?" Granville peeled the lid off a 7-Eleven coffee and slurped. "Some uptown mall? Check out the juvies pulling wheelies on their boards?"

"Mostly Baltimore. But I was occasionally sent

out on assignment from the home office. When I begged enough. I worked stakeouts in Atlanta, LA, Philly, and a terrible two weeks in Mexico City."

Granville took his time fitting the lid back on. "You carry?"

"No."

"What, you got a thing against guns?"

"I figure if I need a weapon, I can find something local."

"You got that right." He slurped again. "Open the glove box, tell me what you see."

Paul did as he was told. He did not need to remove the pistol from its well-worn holster to reply, "Remington thirty-eight, short-action trigger, eleven in the clip and another in the chamber."

Granville nodded, and Paul assumed he had passed the man's form of preliminary inspection. "Okay, our target is the house across the street and two doors down."

"You have binocs?"

Granville slipped a small pair from his jacket pocket. Zeiss. Professional grade. Paul had used them before. He adjusted the clarity, and the house jumped into view. "Reinforced steel overlay on the front door. You've got to assume they've armored the door frame as well. Barred windows, shutters on the inside. Two kids on bikes doing guard duty."

"Actually, the kids are the sales staff," Granville corrected.

"What are they dealing?"

"Rock and meth and coke and the big H. They cover all the bases."

Paul scanned the scruffy yard. "Motion detectors and infrared cameras covering the perimeter."

"I didn't see those."

"They're there."

"You sure about that?"

"Yes." Paul continued his scan. "Are they cooking?"

"No idea. Probably."

"So call your friends on the force and take them out."

"There's a problem."

Paul watched a Porsche Cayenne pull up to the kid on duty to the right of the house. The window rolled down. A yuppie in a striped dress shirt and power tie and suspenders offered a bill to the kid, who exchanged it for a trio of plastic bags. The window went up and the Cayenne drove away. The kid went back to lounging on his fancy banana seat, the gold chains bumping on his little chest as he rocked to the beat on his iPod. He could not have been over ten years old.

Granville went on, "Soon as they moved in, I went downtown and had a word with my buddies. They said they'd take care of it pronto. So I waited. And nothing happened. I went back downtown. I had another word. And I was told to back off."

Paul lowered the glasses.

Granville pointed down the street. "Four houses down on your left. The place with the old Plymouth covered by weeds."

Paul lifted the binocs and gave it a careful inspection. "I don't see anything."

"They're in there."

"Who?"

"DEA. Four months they've had this place on surveillance. Looking for a connection to the biggie. They want to ID the people controlling central Florida's drug trade."

Paul felt his anger building. Four months. With a church and a school and a day-care center and a teen outreach operating under a mile away.

Granville went on, "In that time, the neighborhood's problems have gone out of control. We've got the worst kind of people moving in. This house you're looking at has become the eye of a hurricane. And the leading edge is sweeping up the most vulnerable of the kids in our church programs."

"That is not going to happen."

"It *is* happening. Right *now* it's happening. A lot of the kids Lucy is trying to reach, they could go either way. They come to the church looking for safety and afraid to trust anyone. Then what happens? Dealers start pitching their tent across the street, the women start walking the block between the church and where these kids live, and they think, *No way, this church thing is as bogus as all the other promises society made me and never kept.* And they go over to the dark side. Some have started dealing out of the church's parking lot. Which means sooner or later the church elders, the ones who didn't want us opening this outreach center in the first place, will go ballistic. And everything Lucy's crew is doing will be lost."

Paul felt the icy grip clench his gut more tightly still. "No, what I meant was, I will *not* let this go any further."

Granville had a fleshy, pockmarked face that looked uncomfortable with a smile. "So what's just another retired cop from Baltimore going to do about a drug gang protected by the DEA?"

Paul pointed forward with his chin. "Drive us on back to the church. I need to make a couple of calls."

— Chapter 5 —

Amy vanished in plain sight. She got straight to work, ignoring the people who stared at her through the storefront windows. Because she pretended they did not exist, after a while they did the same for her. Amy sketched out the designs, then drew a pastel overlay on the first three. She stepped back and surveyed her work. It was approaching two in the afternoon. Her back and arms and shoulders ached. She had not stopped for lunch or even a drink of water.

Now came the difficult part.

Amy returned to the owner's outer office. The elderly secretary gave her a frosty look and wrinkled her nose at the odors Amy carried in with her—turpentine and paint and sweat from a hard day in the Florida sun. "Can I please have a minute of Mr. Denton's time?" Amy asked.

The secretary opened her mouth to speak, but Mr. Denton called through the open door, "Be right with you!"

The secretary was in her late sixties and looked to Amy like a plant that had grown roots into the carpeted floor. She sniffed at Amy and typed furiously at her computer. Bob Denton came out wearing his big smile and said, "What can I do you for?"

"I just thought you'd like to have a look at my designs before I start laying the first coat."

"Sure, sure. Hey, have you met Shirley? This is Amy, I'm sorry, I forgot—"

"Dowell. Amy Dowell. Nice to meet you."

"Shirley's been with us since my father sat in that office. She's retiring tomorrow. And we'll miss her a lot."

Shirley sniffed again and continued typing. As

37

they left the office, Bob said, "I've been running this place for twenty-three years, and Shirley still treats me like I'm in short pants and a bow tie."

Amy followed the boss through the new-car showroom. She had studied the salespeople through the window. Most of them were her age or younger. But the way they acted—the jocular chatter, the pranks, the loud hellos and bravado—left Amy feeling a generation older.

The afternoon sunlight was strong and made seeing her designs difficult. Amy had expected this and walked the company owner to the shade of the entrance overhang. "I thought I'd do a rainbow over the doorway here, with cars blooming from the pots of gold at each end."

"This is great. Did you do this for Vickers?"

"No, actually, it came to me when I saw your ads in the local paper, you know, the ones with the 'bright shiny day' logo. I plan to replicate that logo on the windows to either side of this display."

He turned from the windows. "You checked out our ads?"

"Well, sure, Mr. Denton, I wanted—"

"Call me Bob."

"I wanted to do a professional job."

"I wish I could get that sort of professionalism from my sales staff. You know what research they do before they apply for a job? Zip. They think if they can name the models, they're golden. And here you are, checking out my ads just to paint my windows."

He was giving her that stare again. And a couple of the people inside the showroom were noticing. "All part of the service, Mr. Denton."

"Have dinner with me."

"I don't think that's a good idea." When he looked ready to press his case, she added a gentle note of firmness to her voice. "Thank you, but no."

He was so disappointed that he actually deflated. Slumped a bit and scuffed the pavement. "I'm too old for you, aren't I?"

She smiled for all the faces turned their way. "I better get back to my work, Mr. Denton. Thanks for your time."

An hour later, she reentered the office and told Shirley she was breaking for an early dinner and received another sniff in response. The door to Bob Denton's office was closed, and the boss did not show himself. Amy jogged back to her truck and hightailed it to the church. She arrived ten minutes past the day-care center's closing time of four o'clock. When she rushed into the center, she found Kimmie playing on the floor of Lucy's office, building a house out of wooden blocks. "I'm so sorry."

"For what? Your daughter is an angel who's captured our hearts."

"Look, Mommy." Kimmie held up a battered

39

doll that obviously had come from the day-care toy chest. "The baby's gonna have a nap in her new home."

For some reason the words made Amy's eyes burn. She knelt on the floor beside her daughter and said, "Where she's going to be safe and happy."

"And no big bad trucks are gonna come and eat her."

"They don't eat you, honey."

"That's what they sound like." She made a growling sound. "I hate it."

Amy stroked the soft hair. "I know you do."

Lucy asked, "How long have you been on the road?"

"Almost nineteen months. A lifetime." Amy kept stroking her daughter's hair. "I thought it would be a couple of weeks."

"I believe I've heard that before."

"The biggest problem is, the longer we lived in the camper, the more trapped we got. Every cent I earned was spent before it came."

"Making a deposit on a place is impossible," Lucy filled in. "And the unexpected expense leaves you helpless."

"My little darling got a fever five months after we started this life," Amy remembered. "Three trips to the ER, some tests, and the last of our savings was gone. Since then, the thought of what happens next time wakes me up most nights."

Lucy gave that a moment, then asked, "You ready to sign some forms?"

Amy smiled through the liquid veil covering her gaze. "In blood, if you like."

"My plastic pen will do fine, thank you very much."

Lucy led her through an array of documents. There were several for the apartment and another for the power company's deposit, which the church would front but expected her to repay. Amy responded by pulling out the envelope holding her first check from Denton Chevrolet. Lucy smiled approval and pulled out bank forms to open a bank account. "We run a full-service operation here."

There were some forms that the church elders required, which were intrusive but necessary. First was an agreement for the center to access her police and court records. Then there was a form requiring her to have blood tests within three days, and another informing her that she would be subject to random drug tests. Amy signed happily.

Lucy walked her through the rules and regulations governing the apartment, which was hers for a maximum of nine months. Amy tried hard to concentrate, but her mind kept returning to those two amazing words. *Nine months.* She wanted to pick up her little girl and do a dance down the central corridor.

"Mommy, I'm hungry."

Lucy opened her bottom drawer and pulled out a couple of cereal bars. "I've got raspberry and peanut butter."

"Kimmie loves peanut butter better than anything, don't you, honey?"

"Mommy says I'd eat peanut butter on liver if she let me."

Her daughter scooted up into Amy's lap and held the doll with one hand while she ate the bar with the other. As Lucy was starting back on the regulations, there was a knock on her door. "Come."

A burly man with a pockmarked complexion and very kind eyes opened the door. He was also a cop. Amy knew the look and the movement and the smell. All too well. "Got a minute?"

"Sure." When Amy started to rise, Lucy motioned for her to keep her seat. "Amy Dowell, meet Granville Burnes. He runs our church's security team. Amy and her daughter are moving into unit eight."

"Good to meet you, Amy. I hope you'll be very happy here."

Amy wondered if there would ever be a time when she could be comfortable around the police again. "Thank you, Mr. Burnes."

"Call me Granville."

Amy picked a corner off her daughter's cereal bar. Her throat was dry, and her stomach congealed around the tension that every cop caused her these days. She took the food because it gave her something to concentrate on.

Granville said to Lucy, "I took our guest over, like you said. Gave him the ten-cent tour."

"What's your take on Paul Travers?"

"Jury's still out. But he's not wasting any time. He's over in the conference room, pacing and talking on his phone. Got all steamed up when I told him about the feds blocking our way. You want my opinion, I don't see what good another cop on permanent vacation can do for us. But my buddy, the pastor in Baltimore, said this guy was the real deal."

Lucy responded with a shrug. "Doubtful he'll shift this mountain. But I don't see what choice we have. Who is he calling?"

"He said it was best I didn't know. Spent too much time with the feds, you ask me. All smoke and secrets."

When the cop let himself out, Amy risked a glance. The glass wall opened onto the side corridor. On the hall's opposite side was a narrow conference room, where the handsome man she had seen at breakfast talked into a cell phone and jabbed the air with his free hand.

"He's a hunk," Lucy declared.

"He's also a cop." Amy went back to picking another crumb off her daughter's cereal bar. His being a former fed simply meant the load of trouble he could bring down was bigger. She said, "I need to go get something hot for Kimmie's dinner. Then I have to go back to work."

"You're pulling a double shift?"

"There are no shifts. This job needs to be finished by Saturday morning. It pays twelve hundred dollars. I'll sleep when it's done. I'll put Kimmie down in the cab and park on the lot."

"There's no need. We have another two families working night shifts. They'll bed their kids down in the day-care bunks. Kimmie's welcome to join them."

Kimmie piped up, "I want to stay here, Mommy."

Amy found her throat clenched up tight. "All right, sweetheart."

When her eyes cleared and she glanced over, Lucy was watching her with genuine approval. "Something tells me you're going to be just fine."

"I wish there was some way to thank you—"

"Get back on your feet, make a stable home for your daughter, climb out of your hole, keep your feet on the path." The words came out like a well-used chorus. "That's all the thanks I *ever* need."

Amy rose to her feet, Kimmie clinging limpet-like to her neck. She asked, "Can the blood tests wait until next week?"

"You ever do drugs, Amy?"

"No. Never."

"Next week will do fine. Go earn some money

and then get some rest. We stocked your fridge and your pantry. All part of the welcome."

Amy stopped again by the door, turned back, and asked, "Are we going to be friends?"

Lucy's smile lit up the room. "I thought we already were."

As they passed through the exit and crossed the parking lot, Kimmie asked, "Are we going to our new home, Mommy?"

Amy stared upward and blinked fiercely. Above the tired buildings and the pitted asphalt and the spiderweb of power lines was just another Florida sunset. She had never seen anything so beautiful in her entire life. "Yes, sweetheart. We are."

— Chapter 6 —

When Amy returned to work, a new shift of salespeople had taken over. The evening sales staff were entirely different from the day people. The first time she had observed such a change, it had frightened her. Now she knew this was typical for most city dealerships. Most senior sales staff didn't bother with the early-morning traffic. They came in late and did the deals with the people coming off work. The people with money. The people in a hurry. What she saw of most late-shift salespeople, she did not like.

They glanced her way and they shot their cuffs

and they slicked back their hair and they paraded around. They made certain Amy noticed how well dressed they were and how they laughed like winners and how lucky she'd be to have any of them snap their fingers at her. She had learned to put such men down fast and hard. Sometimes it was enough for her to give them *the look*. The one that promised to double any trouble they tried to give her.

When the first of them started her way, Amy stopped and straightened and glared and used her leveling rod to point the guy away. She mouthed one word: *Don't*. The guy must have seen the message in her eyes, because he smirked and strolled past her, shouting a hello to a fellow rising from his car. As if he had never planned to put the moves on Amy. She resumed her painting.

The boss came back around eight that evening. Bob Denton did a slow circuit of the desks out on the salesroom floor. He spent some time with his manager, whose glass-fronted office was next to Denton's. He was drawn into a couple of negotiations, the last one not ending until almost ten. Then he went home. He did not glance at Amy once. She was sorry about that and wished she could have been gentler about the turndown. She had no interest in going out with him. But Bob Denton seemed like a genuinely nice man. She liked how he treated everyone with a grave respect. Amy pushed the thoughts away and returned to her work. She needed the money. And the last thing she had room for was a man.

Just before closing, the showroom saw a flurry of business. There were three quick purchases of Corvettes, all handled by the salesman who had started to put the moves on her. The customers raised her hackles so much that Amy shifted around to the farthest window, in the back, where she could hide. They wore shades and slick gym gear emblazoned with emblems from professional sports teams. They came with their entourages, eight people in all, five women and three men. The men wore tight-brimmed velvet homburgs over do-rags, with big watches and bigger scowls. The ladies were beautiful and hard and deadly. One of the women noticed Amy and walked over to stand on the window's other side. Her clothes cost more than Amy's camper. She had a diamond in her nose and a lot more diamonds on her wrist. She smirked down at where Amy crouched, pretending to paint the window's bottom corner. She mouthed at Amy, *What you waiting for, girl?*

Amy packed up her paint and brushes and left. Behind her, she thought she heard laughter floating over the traffic noise.

She went down the road to a 7-Eleven and treated herself to a cup of coffee and a doughnut. She gave it forty-five minutes, then returned to her work. As she'd hoped, the lot was quiet. The only sign of life was the security guard doing slow circuits on his modified golf cart. He must have been alerted to Amy's presence, for he asked her name, then offered her a gentle hello and continued on his way.

She finished the rainbow arching over the main entrance just after three in the morning. By that point, her body ached and her vision was going a little fuzzy. But she had learned to go a lot longer than this without sleep. She moved away from the main windows and left that more public work for later, after she'd gone back for a nap and a meal. She could sleep two hours and wake refreshed, as long as she had fifteen minutes with her little girl. She moved down to the last window in the direction opposite where she'd been hiding. She started to sketch out the design she was going to use, a starburst with "sale" written inside the center.

Then she saw the money.

The sales force had desks spaced around the showroom floor. On the desk closest to her rested two stacks of bills, possibly more. She could not be certain exactly how much was there because the stacks were covered by a mass of papers. Each of the stacks was over an inch thick. She could see the money only because of her position, crouched at the one angle where the cash was visible under the mound of forms.

Amy knew instantly what had happened. The entourage had paid for their three cars with cash. The salesman had been rushing around, trying to complete the transactions before the close of business. He had walked out with the buyers, laughing and joking, and forgotten the money. It was amazing, especially to her. But she knew how things could get at the end of a long shift. Mistakes happened.

Amy jerked at the sound of voices and slamming doors. She straightened as though she had been caught doing something wrong.

She turned around and saw that the company's cleaning crew had arrived. Four women and one grumpy man stumped past her, headed for the entrance.

Her heart went into overdrive at the prospect of what might happen next. She could just see the cleaners working their way through the room and coming upon the cash. And pocketing it.

If she alerted the security guy to the cash, maybe he would be honest. Maybe. But an hourly-wage grunt staring down at a wedge of cash, there was no telling.

All they had to do was look around for somebody to take the blame.

The sign painter. The stranger. The woman living in a camper.

The nightmare flashed behind her wide-open eyes. The cops. The court. The cold-faced people taking away her little girl. Her life crashing down around her.

All the fears she had tried her best to pray

away from them both, all the threats to their meager and fragile world, all of it bundled together and filled her with molten dread.

Amy was up and moving before she had worked through what was happening. She dumped the contents of her backpack on the sidewalk, the brushes and tins of paint clattering as they fell. Then she ran.

The cleaners backed up in alarm as she rushed up. The guard, however, just glanced over. He was tired, and it was coming up to the end of another long and empty shift. Amy said, "Can I use the little girl's room?"

The guard finished unlocking the main doors and said, "Five minutes."

"Less," Amy promised. But to her dismay, she realized the ladies' room was on the opposite side of the showroom from the desk. She fiddled around inside the ladies' room for a moment, hopping from foot to foot, desperately searching for a reason to get over there.

When she emerged, she saw where a doorway on the showroom's other side opened into a staff canteen. Amy scurried back over to where the guard waited. He was leaning against the door, half asleep, which she took as a good sign. She gave him her number one smile and said, "Mind if I get a cup of water?"

The smile must have worked, for he said, "Knock yourself out."

"Thanks." She rushed away. The kitchenette held a table and a punchboard and a cupboard and a fridge. Amy unzipped her backpack and took a trio of very hard breaths. She poised inside the room for an instant, like a runner getting ready for the starting gun. She shot a quick glance around the doorway. The cleaners were singing from some back office, and the guard had his back pressed against the door, his cap pushed down over his eyes.

Her heart in her mouth, Amy scampered toward the desk. Her rubber soles squeaked so loudly on the polished stone floor that she feared the whole world would hear. She reached under the papers and snagged the bills and jammed them into her pack. One packet, two, three, four, then a fifth. She fumbled with the zipper, then made sure the papers were in more or less the same state as when she'd arrived.

She flew back to the entrance. "Thanks. That's a thousand percent better."

"No problem."

She went back over to her workstation and started gathering up her paints. Her hands shook so hard that she spilled the blue and the indigo over the pavement. She did her best to wipe it up but in the end decided it would have to wait.

She had to get out of there.

— Chapter 7 —

Amy got hardly any sleep. She woke Kimmie at five fifteen and dressed her as she would a limp doll. Kimberly had grown used to unusual hours and put up with the treatment with a few soft whimpers. Amy poured a bowlful of Sugar Puffs, which she fed to Kimmie one spoonful at a time, sipping her coffee in between bites. She showered and dressed in her last set of clean clothes. She needed to do some washing. The studio apartment shared a laundry with the other units, a treasure that Amy intended to enjoy as soon as she had a free moment.

Unless, of course, they ended up getting kicked out this morning. The fear was so great that Amy had to fight against tremors just to lock her door.

Lucy was there when she entered the center. She took one look at Amy and said, "You did right, calling me."

"I didn't know where else to turn. I'm so sorry."

"Don't be. My number is there on the forms for a reason."

"Still, as hard as you work—"

"Amy, look at me," Lucy said sternly. "Yesterday you asked if I was your friend. This is my answer."

She used the hand not holding Kimmie to cover her eyes. "I'm so scared."

"I know you are."

"I've been praying for a chance to give Kimmie a home for nineteen months. The harder I've prayed, the further we've gotten from that. Now you give us a place, and what happens—"

"But you are faced with an impossible situation. And you did the right thing. You came to people who are joined with you in the Spirit."

Kimmie's sleepy voice said, "Mommy, why are you crying?"

Amy wiped her face. "Mommy is tired, honey. But it's okay. We have friends to help us."

"That's right, you do." Lucy reached out. "Give me the angel and go clean your face. We're on in ten minutes."

When Amy returned from the washroom, she found the retired cop in Lucy's office. The previous night, when Amy had phoned Lucy for help, the center director had told Amy she needed to bring in Granville Burnes, their head of security. Amy had been so tired and so frantic that she had not objected. But seeing Granville standing by the doorway, hearing his rumbling voice echoing through the glass wall, caused Amy's fear to notch up even higher. No one knew police officers like a homeless person. The risks she had faced, the terror she had known over having Kimmie taken from her, remained branded upon her soul.

Granville Burnes was talking, and Lucy was frowning at the fed seated in the vacant office next door. Lucy spotted Amy and waved her inside. Reluctantly, Amy switched her little girl to the other hip and entered, her eyes nailed to the floor by her feet.

Lucy greeted her, then said to Granville, "Explain to me what Travers is doing here."

"I told you. We've been on foot patrol."

"That tells me precisely nothing. Kimmie, have you had breakfast?"

"Mommy fed me," Kimberly announced.

"I'm sure she did, honey. Your mommy takes good care of you, doesn't she? If only she did the same for herself." Lucy opened her lower drawer. "Does your mommy like peanut butter as much as you do?"

Amy said, "I'm not hungry."

"Hush up, now, and eat this. You're pale as a sheet, and I bet you didn't sleep any. Sit down over there." Lucy glared Amy into the chair, then turned her ire back to Granville. "I'm still waiting for an explanation."

The big man was untouched by Lucy's irritation. "I don't know what good Paul Travers can do. But I like him."

Lucy leaned back in her chair. "This from the man who said we were probably foolish, bringing in an outsider."

"Won't be the first time I was wrong." He hooked a thumb back at the guy lounging in the empty office. "Travers spent hours on the phone. Talking to one suit after another. Getting more riled by the minute. When I asked him what he was doing, he said pushing against the Washington mountain and remembering what he hated about the system. Around nine last night, I dropped him off at his motel. He asked if I could pick him up at four. Like we were partners working a case. No concern for the hour. Just going after what needs getting done."

Lucy crossed her arms and studied the man through the connecting glass wall. Amy peeled a fragment from the cereal bar and risked a glance. Paul Travers had sprawled out on a lumpy old sofa with his head on the frayed armrest. If he noticed their inspection, he gave no sign. His knit shirt was stretched taut over a muscled frame. He had a small scar on his neck and another above his eyebrow. His hair was dark, his expression stern.

Lucy said, "He told me yesterday that he saw action in Baltimore. I've heard it's a pretty tough place."

Granville kept his gaze on Lucy. "When I asked him about it, he said the only results that counted were the ones in this case."

Lucy liked that, Amy could tell. "So you went on patrol. At four in the morning."

"Paul wants to establish a security perimeter around the church. He wants it to be in place when the bad guys wake up. He wants them to waltz over and find us waiting for them. He's downloaded a detailed map of the area and drawn this circle around our church. In three days, he wants to move out another block. Three days more, another block."

"Cleaning up as you go," Lucy said. "You have the manpower?"

"I called in some friends. Counting the church security, we're fourteen. Enough to work around the clock. At least for a while." Granville glanced through the glass wall. "I should have thought of this myself."

"What happens next?"

"He's got something in mind. Something big. But he won't tell me—"

Granville stopped because his pocket started buzzing. He pulled out his phone, checked the readout, said, "It's Bob Denton."

Amy pressed a hand to her stomach. She wished she had not eaten. She felt nauseated. And cold. And sweaty. All at the same time.

As Granville answered his phone, Lucy murmured, "Steady, girl."

Granville cut the connection. "Bob's outside."

Lucy shifted Kimmie so she could reach out both hands. "Let's take this to the Lord."

— Chapter 8 —

They dropped Kimmie off at day care and moved over to the conference room. Paul Travers rose to his feet as they passed the office where he waited. He solemnly accepted Lucy's thanks for his efforts, then excused himself to go make another round of the perimeter. He had a soft voice, but Amy heard the underlying strength, and it caused her to shiver in fear. Or perhaps it was just the prospect of what was about to come.

"Bob Denton has been in a Bible study with Granville for years," Lucy said once they were seated at the conference table. "Bob also helped finance the apartments where you're living. He sits on the board of my center. I've known him as long as I've been in this position, which is longer than I care to remember."

Amy knew the center director was just filling the empty air and wished she could think of something to say, some way to make it all go away.

"Look at me, girl." When Amy raised her gaze, Lucy went on, "You haven't done anything wrong. I know you're scared. But we are all friends. Including Bob Denton."

"I need this job," Amy whispered.

"That is not—" Lucy focused on something beyond Amy's shoulder. "Here they come."

Bob Denton looked somehow different here, in the church. His ruddy complexion was much clearer in the cheap fluorescent lighting. He wore the same jacket as yesterday, one shade off navy, with gray pants and a pale blue shirt and striped silk tie. He was neat and tall and lean, with short gray hair that looked carefully trimmed. His eyes were somewhere between gray and blue. Amy found it easier to look at him when he wasn't gaping at her. Now he was the one who looked confused and uncertain.

Once again, she found herself calming down. As though something about the man granted her the ability to set aside her normal nerves. She had never considered herself an anxious person. But nineteen months on the street had changed her in many different ways, none of them welcome.

"Good morning, Bob. You know Amy Dowell."

"What's going on here?"

"Please have a seat. We have a serious matter to discuss with you."

Bob Denton looked as if he wanted to object, but Granville kept a hand on his shoulder and guided him into a seat. Denton protested, "Look, you've got to understand, I didn't mean anything untoward by what I said."

Granville and Lucy shared a look of utter confusion.

Bob went on, "I just asked the lady out for a

meal. You folks know me. I wouldn't dream of doing anything wrong."

Granville's face creased in an odd manner, and Amy realized he was holding back a grin. Lucy said quietly, "That's not why we're here, Bob. And nothing is wrong, at least nothing like that. We're not here to complain about anything. We're here to help you."

Bob looked from one to the other. "I have no idea what you're talking about."

"All right, Amy."

Amy opened her pack and pulled out the first bundle of cash. She hated how her hands wouldn't stop trembling. "This is yours."

He reached over and fumbled with the bills. "What—"

"It's all there," Amy said as she laid the other four bundles on the table between them. "Every dime."

"Tell him what happened," Lucy said.

So she did. About working on the window and spying the money on the salesman's desk. And being fearful that the cleaners or the security guy would take it and she'd be blamed. And going inside while the cleaners were there, grabbing the money, and coming back and phoning Lucy. Twice she had to stop and swallow hard against the nausea and the fear.

When she was finally done, Lucy asked, "Did you count the money?"

Amy nodded, suddenly ashamed by the act. "I couldn't sleep."

"How much is there?"

"Four hundred and eighty-five thousand dollars."

"Have you ever held so much cash before?"

"No."

Lucy turned to the dumbstruck Bob Denton and said, "Yesterday I was handling the breakfast counter because our normal lady called in sick. In my quiet time before coming into work, I had the very strong impression that something special was going to happen. Something that would rock my world. That probably sounds silly to you, Bob, but that's how it felt. Like God whispered the words into my ear. Someone is going to come in today and tilt my world on its axis."

"No," Bob murmured. "It doesn't sound silly at all."

"So up pops this beautiful young woman with the sweetest little girl in her arms. She's the one you hear singing over in day care. If a child was ever born to sing, it's Kimberly. And I knew, the first instant I set eyes on the two of them, that these were the people God had in mind.

"So I talk to them, and I learn they've been living rough for over a year and a half. Just the two of them. Clinging to what was left of their family, and clinging to their faith. Over my break-fast talk, I saw her study from my favorite kind of Bible, well worn and filled with underlined passages and scribbling. A Bible used for holding fast to God, even when life had thrown her one hard curve after another. We talked, and I hear she's got a job painting your windows. So I offered her one of our apartments. The same apartments you helped us build. I knew doing this went against the codes you helped us write. About how we had to restrict these places to people we'd gotten to know, or who were referred to us by people we trusted. I had planned to phone you today, after you'd had a chance to meet this woman yourself. I needed to tell you what I'd done, how I'd broken the code I signed my name to, and ask your permission. So that's what I'm doing."

Bob took a long moment to respond. "You're asking my permission to give Amy an apartment?"

"I am. Yes."

"Is this a joke? Of course I agree. After . . ." He turned toward her. "I can't thank you enough."

"You're welcome." To her own ears, Amy's voice sounded as small as Kimmie's.

"Look, I'm in a state of shock, but we've got to do something more to thank you."

Lucy said, "What the lady needs most of all right now is a regular job."

"Absolutely."

"With benefits," Lucy added.

"No problem. I'll make some calls. Happy to."

They chatted for another few moments, Lucy

and Bob and Granville. Amy did not speak again. She kept her gaze on the table by her fingers and reveled in what she had just heard. That Bob Denton was going to keep her on as the sign painter. And perhaps help her find employment. And she and Kimmie could stay in the apartment. All of these bits of good news swirled and coalesced inside her mind and heart. They formed a song, as light and happy as what Kimberly was singing in the next room.

Bob took his leave, thanking Amy again as he left. Granville walked out with him. Amy said, "I better go get ready for work."

"First you and your little girl are joining me for breakfast. No, don't you say a word. I can't make you sleep, but I can make sure you have some hot food."

Amy entered the main day-care room and collected her daughter, glad to have someone to hug. As they entered the hallway, Granville returned and announced, "Bob wanted to make sure it was okay to offer you a reward."

"No . . . I have a place to stay, and he said he'd help me get a job . . ."

"Say yes," Lucy said. She shared Granville's smile.

The former cop pulled a wad of bills out of his pocket. "I believe this is yours."

Amy could not make her hand reach forward.

Lucy asked, "How much is it?"

"Two thousand dollars."

"Go on, girl, take the money." Lucy reached forward and brought Amy's hand up, clearly enjoying herself enormously.

"So much," Amy murmured. Her whole body felt numb.

"You earned it. Now, come on, I'm starving." Lucy shooed them down the corridor. "Nothing like glad tidings to work up an appetite. Granville, you joining us?"

"Nah, I better go make sure Travers is staying out of trouble." He grinned at Kimberly. "That's my good deed for the month. Tomorrow I go back to being the same old grouch."

"He means it," Lucy said.

Amy followed the two of them down the hall. Kimmie kept singing in her ear, as though giving voice to her own joy. But underneath it all was the one unspoken detail. The same fact that had robbed Amy's night of sleep. The one truth that would change everything, wipe away their grins, turn the whole thing sour. And she knew she had to tell them.

Just not yet.

— Chapter 9 —

The salesman who had left the cash on his desk was named Drew. He was the flashy young dresser who had tried to hit on her. Less than half an hour after Amy arrived from the meeting at the church, Drew rammed his Camaro GT into the parking lot and raced into the building. He flung the papers around on his desk, then released a silent scream to the showroom's ceiling.

Bob Denton came out of the office and spoke with him. Amy watched it all through the window. She saw how Drew deflated, then turned and gaped at her through the glass. Her hands were so shaky that she made a squiggly mess of her last rainbow. Fifteen minutes later, Drew pushed through the doors and approached her. Amy tried to plant her brush in the can holding the turpentine and almost turned it over. She clenched her hands and took a very deep breath.

Then she saw how frightened the salesman was. Drew was bone-pale and extremely nervous. "Look, Ms. Dowell—did I get the name right?"

"Yes." She glanced through the showroom window. The entire staff was watching them. Including Bob Denton and the cross woman who was clearing out her desk.

"That was such a totally dumb move," the

salesman said. "Leaving the cash on my desk. It was a rookie mistake."

"Yes. It was."

"I gotta tell you, taking all that cash home and giving it to Bob this morning, that was ace." He fumbled with his wallet.

"Don't. Please."

"You saved my skin, Ms. Dowell." His hands shook so hard that he spilled his credit cards at his feet.

A very curious thing happened then. Amy looked again through the window, really looked, and she realized the people inside were not watching her at all. Their attention was focused on him. Making sure he did the right thing. Seeing this was not what surprised her. Instead, Amy felt as though she looked at the entire world differently. She was no longer the homeless single mother struggling to keep her daughter and make ends meet. She had a home, she had a job, and she had people who were on her side. The sudden calm washed over her like a spring tide. Amy watched him crouch beside where she knelt and gather his credit cards. He had every reason to be nervous. Him. Not her. Amy said, "Mr. Denton already offered me a reward."

"Sure, he told me that." Drew straightened and offered her a sheaf of bills he probably did not even see. "But I want to give—"

"Thank you. But no."

Drew was slender and good-looking, if a lady liked her men flashy and brash and full of themselves. Which Amy definitely did not. He was increasingly tense. Which only heightened Amy's calm. Reluctantly, he stowed his wallet in his pocket. "Look, about that other thing."

Amy took her time rising to her feet. She crossed her arms. Giving him stone. "But there wasn't any other thing. Was there?"

Drew struggled to look beyond his own raw nerves. "What?"

"You forgot to put your money in the company safe. I took it home and brought it back. That's all there is." Amy adopted the hard voice she used when she needed to make sure her five-year-old daughter understood her the first time she spoke. "Isn't that right, Drew?"

"Unh, yeah, sure, I guess—"

"There isn't any guessing here. You were tired. You made a mistake. I helped out. End of story."

"Okayyyy." Drew extended the word so that it lasted through an entire breath. "If you say so."

"Yes, Drew. That is *exactly* what I'm saying." Amy turned away, satisfied that the message had been received. "Now, if you'll excuse me, I'm racing the clock here."

She returned to painting the window and listened to his footsteps. When the front doors rolled open, he turned and looked back. Amy met his gaze. The man was still confused and worried. Which couldn't be helped. Amy returned to her painting.

He knew, and he knew she knew.

The question was, what should she do next?

Amy pushed so hard on completing the last windows that she managed to ignore the stares and the comments. And there were a lot of both. Because everyone knew about her returning the cash. The entire sales staff, all the mechanics, even Shirley. The retiring secretary passed Amy several times, and each time she cast a questioning glance. As if the older woman kept asking herself, *Why did she do it?* Amy had no response to any of them except to keep on working.

Three hours later, she completed the final window. She collected her belongings and started back toward the side street where she had left her truck. The final payment could wait until tomorrow. She was so exhausted that she stumbled over a crack in the sidewalk. Then she rounded the corner, and in a single heartbeat, she went from half asleep to as awake as she had ever been in her entire life.

The woman Amy had last seen through the showroom window leaned against her passenger door. The woman wore another designer outfit, skintight and studded with oversize mother-of-pearl buttons. She had the sloe eyes of a Cajun or mestizo and the hard-edged gaze of a killer. She straightened at Amy's appearance and offered a smile that meant absolutely nothing. "There she is. The lady of the hour."

"What do you want?"

"Oh, I think you know." The woman had a pro's walk, sauntering on high heels like she was on display.

"I don't want any trouble."

"See, that's what I told my man. He was going on about how he needed to get all up in your face, scare you good, maybe take a few licks. And let me tell you, sister. You get hit by my man, you remember it for a long time."

"Get away from my ride."

"Sure thing." The woman took a half step away. "See how agreeable I am?"

Amy dumped her gear in the camper, furious over how her world had been turned upside down again. And angrier still at the returning sense of helplessness. She slammed the door hard enough to startle the other woman. "I asked you a question."

"I'm on your side, girl."

"No, you're not."

"I'm just making sure there won't be any mess going down back there at the car place."

"I already told you." Amy crossed her arms in an attempt to stifle the shakes that emerged with each word. "No trouble."

"That's all I needed to hear. See how easy that is?"

"I don't even see why we're talking at all."

"Just keeping things cool." The woman reached inside her jacket pocket. What she drew out froze Amy's blood.

The knife had many names. Originally, it was known as a Batangas, or a Balisong, after the region in the Philippines from which it came. On America's streets, it was known as a butterfly knife. Two years ago, Amy would not have dreamed she would ever know such things. She watched in horror as the woman began the spinning dance that local gangs called flipping or fanning. The dual handles and the blade shimmered in the light. It was like watching a cobra dance.

The woman smirked. As she turned and walked away, her heels clicked on the sidewalk in time to the blade's spin. "You have yourself a good day now."

— Chapter 10 —

Amy had two cases of the shakes on her way back to the church. The knife flashed, the woman gave her the empty smile, and the tremors worked their way up from her gut and caused the truck to shimmy. She parked over by the apartments, then sat there long enough to bring her breathing under control. This should have been the happiest day she had known in a long while. And that was the face Amy was determined to show her little girl.

When Amy walked down the hall to the day care, Lucy emerged from her office and said, "Your little one is still napping. How did it go at the dealership?"

Amy fought down a ferocious urge to tell her what had happened. But there was no way she could tell part of that story. Telling it all meant cops. So all Amy said was "It went okay."

Lucy cocked her head. "Something wrong?"

The fear and the need forced out a tear. "I'm just tired."

"Understood. Listen, we have a group that meets here tonight. Friends putting their lives back on the right track. There's room for one more."

Amy was about to refuse, but the urge to find strength from others was too strong. "Let me fix the little one dinner and I'll see."

She entered the day care and gently lifted her daughter. Her daughter whined over the smell of Amy's turpentine-stained clothes without fully waking up. Amy unlocked their apartment and settled Kimmie into the big bed, then got in the shower and lingered. The water was gloriously hot and the bathroom was sparkling clean and the towel was fresh. There wasn't any grime on the floor from other unseen visitors. There was no rust in the water or on the taps, the mirror wasn't broken, the sink wasn't stained. Her home.

She stretched out beside her daughter on the bed and stroked the white-blond hair with her paint-stained fingers, thinking she would lie here just a moment, not long, and then she would get up and make her daughter something to eat. Amy did not expect to sleep, but she was so exhausted that she conked out for almost two hours. When she awoke, Kimmie was playing on the carpet by the coffee table, building another house for the doll she had adopted from the church toy box.

"Mommy, you've been snoring."

Amy's entire body complained from the simple act of sitting up. "Baby, why didn't you wake me?"

" 'Cause you were so sleepy."

"But what did you eat for dinner?"

"Froot Loops."

"You made a bowl of cereal all by yourself?"

"Missy helped."

"Who?"

"Missy!" Kimmie held up the battered doll. "She found the peanut butter, too! And the crackers!"

Amy rubbed her face, and her eyes focused to where she could see a packet of open saltines on the coffee table, next to a jar of peanut butter with a knife jammed into the contents. The low table and the floor were covered with a colorful array of cracker crumbs and cereal and milk. "Aren't you my good sweet girl."

She cleaned up the remnants of her daughter's meal while she made herself coffee and a sandwich that she ate standing by the darkened window. Her reflection showed a woman at the very fringe of coming undone. She knew she needed help. But she had spent two grueling years dealing with life alone. It was so hard to ask. Even when people seemed ready to lend a hand.

Amy put pajamas on her daughter and tucked Kimmie into the narrow bed, pulling the sheets up tight to her chin. "Mommy is going out for a while."

"To work?"

"No, sweetheart. I told you. The job is done. I'm going to church."

"To meet with Lucy."

"That's right. And some friends of hers."

"I like Lucy."

"I like her, too." Amy set her cell phone down on the little table next to Kimmie's bed. "If you wake up and need me, what are you going to do?"

"Turn on the phone and hit redial."

"That's my big girl." She had dialed in the number to Lucy's direct line. Amy stroked her daughter's cheek. "Close your eyes and drift off to dreamland."

"It's quiet here, Mommy. I like it."

"I like it, too, honey." She stayed until her

daughter's breathing changed. Then she rose in stages, for her position had been the same as when she was painting the lower segments of the windows. Her back had stiffened, and her thighs were so tired that they trembled. Even so, she gathered up her keys and purse and softly shut the front door behind her.

She needed to do this.

Paul Travers and Granville Burnes spent the day setting up the volunteers, pairing the weak with the strong, ensuring that they could all be relied on to treat the work as real and the threat as genuine. The side wall of Granville's office now held an elongated flow chart, with teams and assignments running out for the next two weeks. The opposite wall held a hand-drawn map of the neighborhood, a mile to a side, with the church at the center. Known hot spots were noted in red, with codes for what the dots signified in case prying eyes came in for a lookie-loo. Paul had continued to field calls, to no avail. The DEA's operation climbed the food chain so high that none of his Washington contacts were able to bring a satisfying response as to why there was no movement on an official protest backed up with hard evidence. In fact, two of his allies had come back with the terse instruction that Paul was not to contact them again. Debt or no debt, this was off-limits.

Granville had not shown any disappointment at Paul's failure. The former cop apparently had answered whatever doubts he might have been carrying. That afternoon he had led Paul from the church, humming a little tune. As they walked another circuit of the new perimeter, he related what had happened that morning when Amy returned the car dealer's money. Twice Granville chuckled as he described the encounter and the woman and her tears over a reward she deserved but had not expected.

They returned to Granville's car and drove to a Venezuelan café. Granville went inside and returned with coffee and breakfast burritos. That was something Paul missed from his days on the force, the gift of food signifying the stamp of friendship. And the all-day-breakfast routine. Cops worked to their own internal clock. That Granville had not asked Paul if he was even hungry suggested the man was ready to treat Paul as an ally.

Granville drove back and parked down the street from the drug house, in the opposite direction from the DEA surveillance team. They peeled the tops off the coffee cups and sipped, and unwrapped the burritos. Two men well used to the quiet spaces between words.

Granville asked, "How much does a new Corvette run these days, eighty thou?"

"I've been thinking the same thing," Paul

replied, and took a bite. There was nothing to compare to a fresh, homemade burrito. His contained two scrambled eggs, chopped tomatoes, white salted cheese, beans, and a bit of spinach. "This is the best meal I've had in a long time."

"Yeah, they're addictive." Granville patted his ample pouch. "Living testimony."

"Four hundred and eighty-five thousand dollars," Paul said. "The amount doesn't add up."

"I asked about that," Granville said. "The salesman claimed the extra was down payment for a couple of vans."

"But the way he left all that money on his desk . . ."

When Paul didn't go on, Granville said, "Finish your thought."

"The man's mind was elsewhere," Paul said. "As in, seriously taken by whatever brought in the cash."

"Seriously stoned, more like," Granville agreed. "This smells like a lot more than just a cash purchase of three very expensive sports cars."

"What if the buyers didn't just waltz in off the street and choose this guy at random?" Paul said, thinking aloud. "What if they had this arranged in advance? And their salesman is known to them. Because he's a client for the dope they're dealing. So they come in, they buy the cars, they leave a lot more cash than the cars are worth. But by this time, the salesman has taken a couple of trips outside with his clients, and they've done a lot more than race the car engines. So he's well and truly toasted, and he leaves the cash there on his desk."

"It's the only reason I've come up with for how that money ended up lying there," Granville agreed.

"Which brings us to the question you don't want to ask yourself." Paul finished his burrito and wished there were more. "If they're laundering money, it's going to take more than the one inside guy."

"Which is why I wanted to see Amy hand the money back," Granville confirmed. "I've known Bob Denton since my early days on the force. He's totally stand-up. We've been through a lot. The loss of both our wives, problems with his only son. He's the only civvie I've ever talked with about my bad days on the force."

"How did it look to you?"

"He was caught completely off guard. There was nothing behind the surprise except gratitude. I'd stake my pension on Bob Denton being totally clean."

"So what do we do now?"

Granville nodded slowly, as though he had been wondering the same thing and had come to a decision. "I need to swing by the station, have a word with an old pal. Want to come along for the ride?"

· · ·

The city of Brentonville hid its beauty well. The northern part, the section where the church was located, merged into the sullen underbelly of Orlando. But farther south stood an entirely different town. The traffic slowed; the roads became lined by trees and blooming hedges. The homes were as well tended as the lawns. Paul lowered his window and listened to birdsong and children's laughter. In the distance he glimpsed the glistening waters of a palm-lined lake.

They entered an old-fashioned business district. People strolled and chatted. Granville pulled into a spot on the street and fed the meter. A pair of English spaniels on leashes offered Paul a tail-wagging welcome while the woman leading them spoke with Granville. He introduced her as a member of his Sunday school class. Paul did not catch her name. She invited Paul to join them the next day and departed. The dogs sniffed his hand one final time and trotted along beside her. Paul asked, "You teach Sunday school?"

"The other guy kicked the bucket. They asked. I've always had trouble saying no to the church."

They walked the entire three blocks of the business district, then crossed the street and retraced their steps. Paul knew the purpose was to introduce him to Granville's home, the town under threat, the reason the man would remain a cop as long as he drew breath. Paul liked Granville even more for taking the trouble to explain without words.

The police station was tucked down a side street, hidden from the shopping district by the courthouse and the city's largest office building. Granville greeted officers with the ease of a cop who'd never truly left the force. They were buzzed through the back door, walked a hall past offices and interview chambers, and entered the bullpen. Granville led Paul to a desk by a window and introduced him to Consuela Sanchez. The detective was compact and sturdy and examined Paul with a pro's cold distance.

Granville said to Paul, "Tell her what you're thinking."

Paul knew the former cop did not need him to detail the past twenty-four hours. Granville was using this as an opportunity for his ally on the force to make her own assessment of this stranger. Paul gave it to her in terse bites—the frustrating calls to Washington, the contact with Amy Dowell, the money, the questions.

When he was done, Consuela continued to study him. She wore her hair as short as a man's, which accented the strong angle to her jaw and the sharp slant to her dark eyes. "You were a cop?"

"Federal agent. Based in Baltimore. Five years."

"You mind if I make a few calls of my own?"

"It's what I'd do."

"So why'd you leave the force?"

He gave her the bare minimum. "Took a bullet. Medical discharge. Burnout and a bad divorce."

"Sorry."

He nodded, glad she did not press.

"So now, what, you go around helping out churches with problems?"

"Something like that."

Consuela tapped her pen on the notepad. "It doesn't add up. Four hundred and eighty-five thousand dollars isn't enough of a reason for the feds to shut us out."

Paul liked how she honed in on the one crucial element. It meant she accepted him, at least enough to discuss the case. "That's been bothering me, too."

"I'll ask around, see if anyone's heard something about Denton Chevrolet being linked to the money flow."

"But discreetly," Granville warned. "We don't want to spook them."

"You trained me, remember?" She rose to her feet and said to Paul, "That was smart, forming a ring of guards around the church and moving outward."

"Thanks." Paul shook her hand, which was surprisingly small and hard as granite. "Sooner or later, we're going to step on the DEA's toes."

Her smile was there and gone in an instant.

"I'm counting on it. And I want to be there when it happens."

The two men wound their way back through the station and out the main exit. Granville settled behind the wheel, started the car, then hesitated, showing uncertainty for the first time that day. "You got anything planned for tonight?"

"I thought I'd walk the beat, check on the teams, grab a bite."

"This isn't work-related. Lucy runs a group at the church; they meet three evenings a week."

"You mean like AA?"

"Same tactic, different issue. I've been attending for a couple of months. The aim is to help folks who've gone through a hard time get their life back on track." He pulled the keys from the ignition and rolled them like worry beads. "I lost my wife four years ago. Spent a long time pretending I could handle it alone. Too long. The group's helped me a lot. I just thought—"

"You thought right," Paul said, surprising them both. "I'd like to come. A lot."

— Chapter 11 —

But as the time approached, Paul became increasingly unsettled. It was one thing to hear a fellow cop talk about opening up to friends; it was another to actually do it himself. Paul had never been good at confession, not even to his wife. Every agent he knew was taciturn when it came to work and personal issues. The two seemed to go together. Frontline forces learned never to discuss their work at home. Opening up about the experiences meant sharing the risks they took. And their spouses and families were already worried. So they didn't talk. Clamming up became second nature. So what was he doing, agreeing to come to this session?

The answer was simple enough: His life wasn't working.

He felt good about projects like this one. His disability pension was enough to cover his living expenses. His ex-wife was remarried to an orthodontist; they had a daughter and another child on the way. She had never been one to pester him, and occasionally they chatted like people who once were friends. Paul knew he'd been the problem. He was drifting. And not just from city to city, job to job. His work only reflected his restless nature. In the dark hours when he could not sleep, he felt the gnawing hunger of an unfulfilled life. That was why he had agreed to join Granville. He was desperate for answers.

But as he followed Granville down the church hall, he wished he had shown the good sense to stay away.

Paul's misgivings were made worse when Lucy hit him with her heat-seeking gaze before he even entered the room. She rose and halted them both with an angry "What's going on here?"

Granville Burnes replied, "I invited him. Paul accepted. End of story."

"No, it's not." She crossed her arms. "There are no outside visitors in this group. No spectators."

"I understand."

"So tell me, Paul, I'm interested in why you think you belong here."

Paul knew this confrontation was mostly for the benefit of the others in the room. Lucy wanted them to see he had to earn the right to join them. And do so against her wishes.

He said, "This group wants to get their lives back together. So do I."

She tightened her gaze. "For real?"

"Yes."

"All right." She pointed him to a lonely chair at the table's far end. "Take a seat there."

"Lucy," Granville groused. "Give the guy a break."

"He's here. That's all the break he's getting."

She remained standing as Paul seated himself. "That's what we call the hot seat. You get to shine tonight. Explain to everybody why you think you deserve to be here." She waved her hand at the others. "They get to tell you what they think."

About thirty people crowded around the table and lined the three walls. His side of the table held only one chair. The rest of the people sat shoulder to shoulder. Thirty pairs of eyes gazed at him with overt suspicion. Paul said, "Four years ago I was shot in the line of duty."

A hard-faced black man with a voice as deep as a well asked, "You were a cop?"

"Federal agent."

"Same thing," a woman muttered. "One cop is enough."

Granville shook his head, his acne-scarred cheeks ruddy with genuine irritation. But he didn't speak.

Paul went on. "My wife left me. She said she wasn't going to hang around and wait until the next bullet took me out. I spent the next six months hooked on prescription painkillers. Lost my job to a medical discharge. Didn't care." He had to stop and push through a couple of hard breaths. "I had no idea what to do. But I knew if I didn't find something, I'd swallow either a bottle of the drugs or my gun."

Lucy's tone softened a fraction. "So you started working for churches."

"That's right. I had a friend who was the pastor of an inner-city Baltimore church. He saw me through my divorce. Some days it felt like he was the only person I could talk to. He urged me to find a new direction. Not forget the past, but . . ."

The black man said, "Find a new balance."

Paul nodded slowly, giving his body time to release some of the tension. He tried to tell himself it was right to do this. Confess. Open up. With strangers. Do the impossible—ask for help. "There was a youth ministry run by a friend of his. The pastor suspected his own assistant of drug dealing. And enlisting the kids in their racket."

"Man, that is cold," Granville said.

"I helped them take care of things," Paul said.

"Quietly," Granville said, looking at Lucy. "Nobody needed to know the problem even existed."

"He had a pal in another church with another problem," Paul went on. "And another. And another."

"And now you're here," Lucy said.

"Yes. I am. And I've already got another place that needs me when I'm done here."

The black man had the build of a boxer on the wrong end of too many losses. "How many times you done this, man?"

"This is the eighth church."

"Is there anybody else doing what you do?"

"I don't know of any. But there should be."

"That's not what brought you here tonight, is it?" Lucy said. "This isn't about problems at churches."

"No."

"So tell us the real reason, Paul."

"I'm doing what's right. I've got a job I can get my teeth into. But it's not a life. I feel like I'm drifting from one place to another. I live on the job, but at night, when I go back to my motel room, I turn on the television, and I have no idea what I'm watching. I eat a meal that I don't taste. I sleep sometimes. I get up, I get on with the job. And when it's done—"

"There ain't nothing," the black man said, nodding. "But another dark cave some folks call a life."

Paul found the strength to look up. And found his gaze held not by the man who spoke but by the woman who sat next to him.

Amy Dowell wore an oversize sweatshirt, one large enough for her to pull out and over her knees, tucking her legs up onto the chair with her. She drew the sleeves down so that they covered all but her fingernails. She wrapped her arms around her shins, and she rested her chin upon her knees. She watched him intently, her eyes the pale blue of a rain-washed dawn.

He realized Lucy had spoken to him. "I'm sorry. I don't . . ."

"I asked what you wanted from life."

It was the issue he had spent too many months avoiding. "That's just it," Paul said. He heard the crack in his voice and found that for once he did not mind. "I don't know."

"Which is why you're here."

"I need to know this. I need to understand what comes next. I need to figure out how to . . ."

"How to live," the black man said.

"Yes."

"How to *really* live. How to live like tomorrow means something."

"I've tried to do this alone. And it doesn't work." Paul's voice sounded strange to his own ears, as if it had marched on through time, leading him forward to the point where all the wasted days waited to condemn his futile efforts. "I need help." He sat and sweated and stared at the table between his fists. His whole body felt pummeled, as if he had spent the past few minutes beating at himself.

Then a soft voice from the table's other end said, "I need help, too. With something really private."

— Chapter 12 —

After Lucy had given the closing prayer and dismissed the class, Amy asked if Paul and Granville would remain behind. The whole time she talked, she kept her gaze locked on Paul. No one spoke. Paul found no need to ask questions. The only suggestion he made came right at the start. Amy spoke in fragments, as if the tension in her voice were reflected in fearful bursts of thought. So Paul asked her to go back and start at the beginning. From the moment she first saw the cash.

It was a favorite tactic of many interrogators when dealing with a witness who was so frightened that the events came out disjointed. Taking it from the top opened the conversation and revealed discrepancies. Which Paul doubted they would hear in Amy's words. He was quite certain she was telling the truth. But forming a time line was crucial in establishing a probable chain of guilt, and of evidence.

They sat around the oval conference table. Amy and Lucy sat on one side. Paul sat with his back to the windows overlooking the internal hallway. Granville sprawled two seats farther down, his hands laced over his ample belly. On the surface, Granville looked like a rumpled bear. But his eyes glowed fiercely. Paul knew that light: It was a hunter's gleam, burning when the prey came in sight. Paul felt exactly the same way.

When Amy went silent, Granville shifted, making his chair squeak. "Let me make sure I got this straight. You see the cash lying there. The guy's desk—What's his name again?"

"Drew."

"Last name?"

"I don't know."

"Doesn't matter. Drew's desk is over in the corner of the showroom. Right or left?"

"Looking through the front window, his desk is to the right."

"The cleaners haven't gotten there yet. But they will. So you rush in and grab the loot, and when you do, you find yourself staring at a white powder residue."

"More than a residue. The desk looked like a countertop where the flour has been shaped around making cookies."

"So you decide the only thing to do is to sweep up the powder with the cash."

"Did I do wrong?"

"No," Paul replied. "Not at all. You did exactly right. Leaving it would signify that whoever holds the cash has seen too much."

"If the man was so stoned that he left almost five hundred grand behind, he won't be certain of anything." Granville kept up an easy rumble, as if taking a verbal stroll through the park. "So you've still got it, right? The white stuff."

"Yes." Amy's attention remained focused intently on Paul. As though she could speak at all only because of him. He wasn't sure how it connected to his confession, but he was certain the two were linked. Even though the act of revealing himself left his throat and heart raw, he was glad he had opened up. Amy's gaze was unwavering, almost unblinking. Even now, with Granville leading her through a recap, she watched Paul. As though he were the only man who mattered.

Paul asked, "Is it still in your backpack?"

"No. I cleaned it out. I use my pack all the time to carry my personal effects. I collected all the powder I could, then I wiped down the pack. Twice."

"Where is the white stuff now?"

"In my pocket." She was talking faster. "Lucy said no drugs. So I kept it in the camper. I knew I was going to have to tell somebody. But I just needed a little time, I don't know . . ."

Lucy said softly, "Amy, you haven't done a single thing wrong."

A tear escaped. "I like it here so much."

"I'm glad. You know why?" Lucy reached over and took hold of her hand. "This is your home."

Granville asked, "Can I have the white stuff, please?"

Amy used her free hand to pull out a small plastic bag and slide it across the table.

"Thank you, Amy." Granville made the packet disappear. He eased farther into his chair and tilted his chin until he was addressing the ceiling. As though the room were not crowded with Amy's tension. "So you go back to work today. And this salesman rushes in, searches his desk, talks to Bob, then comes out and offers you cash."

"Which I refused. I couldn't take it. I just couldn't."

Lucy asked, "Does that make a problem?"

Granville pursed his lips, then decided, "I suspect old Drew is so grateful to have his cash back, he's convinced his world is just golden."

Amy said, "I told him there was nothing else to discuss. Ever."

"That's right. You did good." Granville kept talking to the overhead lights. "So you finish the last window. And you walk back to your camper, which is parked . . ."

"One street to the north."

"And there's a lady of the night there waiting for you. You're sure she was the same one you saw in the showroom buying the 'Vettes?"

"She didn't buy them. The guys did."

"You said that already. Good. But you're sure it's her. Even though the desk was . . . how far away from where you were painting?"

90

"Across the showroom. But she came over and spoke to me."

Granville's head came back down. "You didn't say that before."

"She spoke to me through the window. But I understood. Every word."

"What did she say?"

Amy kept looking at Paul as she repeated, " 'Girl, what are you waiting for?' "

Paul could see how close she was to the edge. They had all they needed for the moment. And there was something more that had to be done that night. He rose to his feet and said quietly, "Thank you, Amy. What you've given us may just be the key."

"It's all coming together," Granville agreed. "Thanks to you."

Paul went on, "I really appreciate this gift of trust."

Another tear escaped. Her lips trembled so hard that she mangled the words. "Protect me and my baby. Please."

"That is my first duty," Paul replied. "I'm just a guy trying to help out a church. And you're part of this. You and your daughter."

"But . . . what can you do?"

He turned to Lucy. "If there's an apartment available, I'd like to move in. Tonight."

Lucy was already up and moving before he finished speaking. "Outside. Now."

● ● ●

Lucy led him down the hall far enough to block them from the pair still seated at the conference table. She stepped in close, so Paul could see the glowing embers in her dark eyes. She said, "I can't have you preying on my people."

He could not have been more surprised if she had reached out and slapped him. "What are you talking about?"

"Amy. And don't give me that innocent tone."

"She isn't—That's not it at all."

"You didn't think I'd notice how you two scoped each other out in there?"

"I'm not chasing the lady."

"That's right. You're not. My people are at their most vulnerable when they come in here. The worst thing, the *absolute worst* thing that could happen, would be for her to find some strong, dark knight who offers to make everything right in her world. Because you're not staying. You'll do this job, and then you'll leave. And she'll realize you were just another vulture, only dressed in nicer clothes and talking church talk. And she will think she's not safe here even in the church. She'll decide she's destined to be prey for the rest of her life. She'll strop trusting. And I won't have that. You are *not* becoming part of that woman's problem."

"Lucy, you've got to believe me. Going after Amy is the last thing on my mind."

Lucy cocked her head. "Are you actually blushing?"

He felt the flames inside his skin grow hotter. "I came here tonight for the reasons I said."

She studied him for a long moment before deciding, "You know what? I actually believe you."

Paul was not done. "I had no idea she was going to open up like that. But I'm glad she did. Because until she spoke, we didn't have a clue what we were going to do next."

She took a step back and studied him while the ire faded from her gaze. "It's not often I read a person completely wrong."

He was still so embarrassed that he stumbled over the words. "You're trying to do the best you can for your people."

"That's right, Paul. I am."

"They're lucky to have you. And I'm on your side."

"Granville said I should trust you. I'm beginning to see why. All this time I've been thinking it was us who needed you. Now I'm thinking this might be a two-way street."

The same emotions clawed at his raw throat. "I think so, too."

Lucy offered him what was perhaps her very first genuine smile. "In that case, we've just moved a family into their new home. The apartment two down from Amy is free. You can move in tonight."

— Chapter 13 —

Sunday morning Amy did as the two cops had suggested. She knew Granville was retired, and Paul had been a fed and was now helping the church, but she still thought of them as a pair of cops, two men who had belonged to the group she avoided at all costs. It left her unsettled to dwell on how much rested in their hands. Trusting anyone was very difficult for her these days. And now that was all she was doing. Her future depended upon strangers who claimed to have her best interests at heart.

She dressed in the cotton shift she kept for the Sundays when she and Kimmie were able to attend church. The Internet chat rooms for homeless people trying to keep a hold on life often discussed these places: churches where the faces were friendly and hope was offered with the free coffee. People who genuinely cared. Havens from the hurt and the fear. At least for a morning.

The dress was part of the old life, a nice floral pattern that set off her hair. She let Kimmie wear her favorite pink dress. But as she buckled the straps on her daughter's sandals, Amy observed, "Honey, these shoes are too small."

"They're my favorite, Mommy."

"Look at how they pinch." The sandals were the

same shade as the dress and had sparkly stars painted across the top. "Your toes are squished up like ten little sausages."

"But I *like* them."

Amy shifted back and looked at her daughter. Kimmie's dress had been washed until the seams were fraying. Amy had replaced a loose button with orange thread because it was all she could find. The girl was growing, and the dress was both too short and too narrow in the shoulders. She wore a hair clip that once held a smiling Peter Pan, but the elf was gone and still Kimmie wore it every chance she got. Amy swallowed and said, "My baby girl is growing up."

"Please let me wear them, Mommy."

"Of course, darling." Amy had managed to ignore these things because she had been unable to do anything about them. That was nothing new. What she saw now was how her daughter had learned to do the same. Kimmie ignored her hurting feet because to do otherwise meant giving up something she cherished. Amy wiped her eyes. "What a big, beautiful girl you are."

"I'm still just five."

"How would you like to go shopping for a new outfit this afternoon? Dress and shoes both."

"Pink ones?"

"Any color you like. And if you could have anything in the whole wide world for dinner tonight, what would it be?"

Kimmie's eyes went round. "Can we do that?"

"Anything and everything," Amy said. "We can even go to a restaurant if you like."

"I don't want to go anywhere, Mommy. I like it here."

"I like it here, too. So what do you want to eat?"

She answered as Amy knew she would. "Chickie burgers and tater tots and corn!"

For once, Amy did not insist her daughter have greens. "Did you forget dessert?"

Kimmie's laugh carried a bell-like clarity that caused Amy to shiver. "Nutter Butters and chocklit ice cream!"

Amy led her daughter out of the apartment. Before she shut the door, she took one last look inside. Sunlight spilled through the kitchen window, touching the breakfast plates drying in the rack by the sink. Kimmie's ratty doll was seated on the sofa, waiting for her playmate to come back. Amy's Bible was open on the counter, where she had read it with her coffee. There was a normalcy to the scene. A promise of better things to come. And no one was going to take that from them.

It was good to be home.

The church sanctuary was at the far end of the complex, around the Sunday school building and across two parking lots. Tall imperial palms and blooming oleander framed the structures. As she checked the side road for traffic, she noticed that Paul Travers was shadowing her. The man was dressed, as usual, in a knit shirt and dark pants. He hung back far enough to blend in with the other people headed for church. He wore sunglasses and did not appear to look her way at all. But Amy knew he was there to protect her and found great comfort in the fact that she had been right to trust him.

As she led Kimmie up the stairs and into the large foyer, her mind went back to how Paul had spoken the previous night. The act of confession had burned him, just as it would her. She dreaded opening up in front of others, though she knew it was part of the healing process. Watching Paul do it had left her convinced that she should trust him. That here was someone who would do what he said and be there in the hard moments. She needed friends like that, especially now.

She'd started to slip into an empty pew when she spotted a familiar head two rows up. Bob Denton sat alone. She hesitated just a moment, then walked forward and asked, "Mind if we join you?"

Bob Denton's face lit up at the sight of her, and Amy knew she had done the right thing. "Kimmie, this is Mr. Denton. I've been working for him this week."

"Painting pretty windows," Kimmie said.

"The prettiest in Florida," Bob said, slipping down and making room. "What a beautiful little girl you are."

"Mommy is taking me shopping this afternoon."

Amy fished crayons from her purse and handed them to her daughter. "Kimmie has never met a stranger."

Bob glanced at her, then went back to smiling at her daughter. "What are you going to buy?"

"A new dress and sandals." Kimmie lifted her feet. "Pink ones. As pretty as these."

"You will be cute as the sunrise when you're done."

Amy said, "Thank you, Mr. Denton."

"Call me Bob."

When the service was over, Amy remained seated beside her little girl. It was a habit she had started soon after they hit the road. Amy wanted her daughter to hold on to all the good things that remained within reach. She could not tell such lessons to a child. She had to *show* them. Here was safety. Here was a place where she could feel connected to all the goodness in the world. This was a true sanctuary from life's uneven hand. And Kimmie needed to feel it for herself.

Bob Denton rose with the congregation, but when he saw that Amy remained sitting, he settled back down. Amy started to say he should leave, but Kimmie chose that moment to ask her, "Was this like the church where you and Daddy went?"

Their life before things fell apart was a favorite topic of Kimmie's after church. Amy had disliked it at first but decided it was good for her child to feel safe enough once each week to ask the difficult questions. Even when it made Amy's heart swell up and her eyes burn to reply, "Our church was smaller. But the feeling was the same."

"The church was stone."

"That's right, darling."

"Made from the mountains."

"West Virginia granite," Amy confirmed.

"And Daddy held me."

"You didn't like going into the nursery. You wanted to be with us."

"And I fell asleep."

"Almost every Sunday."

Bob watched this exchange with a somber expression. As Kimmie continued drawing on the church circular, he asked, "What has it been like for you two out there?"

Amy did not need to ask what he was talking about. "Mostly it was about making it through each day. The hardest part was the fear at night. That we wouldn't find a way out."

"A lot of people just give up." Bob followed Amy's lead and kept his voice light. "Lucy says her hardest job in choosing people for the apartments is finding those strong enough to keep hoping."

Amy stroked her daughter's hair. "Thank you for giving us this chance. The home, the job—they are answers to prayers I almost forgot how to say."

Bob took his time replying. He was clearly a man who took his exercise seriously. He stretched out his long legs, slipping his feet under the pew in front of him. His shoes were either new or recently polished, pale brown loafers with woven leather bands across the top. They looked expensive. "When my wife died, I almost did that—forget how to pray. Give up hope. One Sunday I was sitting right here in this very pew. Lucy was there where you are. Afterward we started talking."

Kimmie surprised them by announcing, "I like Lucy."

"I like her, too." Bob responded to Kimmie as he would to an adult. "And that Sunday she was an answer to a prayer, just like you described, one I had almost forgotten how to ask. I needed something more than the business and the routine to make it worth going on. Lucy told me about this decrepit motel that was going into bankruptcy. I knew about it, of course. The whole church despised the place. You know what I'm talking about, right?"

Amy kept stroking her daughter's hair. "They rented rooms by the hour."

"Exactly. Folks had been complaining about this place for years, but Lucy was the first to come up with an idea that was forward-looking. Renovate it into small apartments and combine it with our other outreach programs. She had taken it to the elders and been shot down. She didn't know what to do or where to go. So she had been sitting there, praying over it."

"And you bought it."

"I helped," Bob corrected. "Some friends and I."

"You were the driving force. You made it happen." Amy shook her head. "Someday I might find a way to tell you just how much that place means to us."

"I like it there," Kimmie said.

Bob glanced at his watch. "The next service is about to begin. Want to come with me to Sunday school?"

Most of the class members were older than Amy, but not all. A gray-haired woman found Kimmie some drawing paper and made a game of sneaking three colored markers from Granville's whiteboard. Kimmie sat at the desk used by the greeter and drew. When Kimmie started humming midway through the session, and the women in the class glanced over and shared smiles with Amy, she felt an unseen band of tension ease a notch. As though the really important point of this particular Sunday was learning to set her burdens down.

After class, Bob introduced Amy and Kimmie to the others, then drew her away from the exit and said, "There's a man who's been dogging you."

"I know. Paul Travers."

"You want me to do something about it?"

Granville was the only other person in the room. He made a slow circuit around the class, gathering books and papers, pointedly ignoring them. Amy chose her words carefully. "I might be followed by some bad people. Paul is keeping me safe."

"A pretty girl like you, I can't imagine . . ." Bob stopped when Kimmie walked over, beaming as she offered them her drawings. "Look what a nice picture you've made!"

"Did you and your wife have children?"

"One. A boy." Bob shook his head, closing that subject. "You're certain you can trust this man?"

"Granville does."

The burly cop used his name as an excuse to sidle up. "Paul is a new buddy. He's one of the good guys."

"You're sure about that?"

"More every day."

"Well, I guess that's all right." Bob hesitated, then said, "I've got something I want to talk with you about."

"Me or the lady here?"

"Both, I guess."

"Why don't we take a seat?"

Kimmie protested, "Mommy, I'm hungry."

Amy reached into her pocket for a cereal bar and realized she had forgotten to bring it along. "In a minute, baby."

Bob took that as his cue. He passed over an envelope. "This is the remainder we owe you for the paintings. I've put in a little something extra."

"You don't need to. Really."

"We're already hearing some nice things about your work. We've shot another ad using your paintings as a backdrop. Take the money. You've earned it."

Amy stowed away the envelope. "Thank you. This means the world."

"About your next job. I've made a few calls. Unfortunately, I haven't found anybody who's hiring. The economy here is hurting."

"Sure, like everywhere." Amy told herself there was no reason to feel as disappointed as she did. "Thanks to your generosity, we've got a bit of a cushion. I'm sure something will turn up."

Bob fiddled with his tie. "How'd you like to come work for me?"

Amy did not understand why asking her that question made him so nervous. "You mean do another mural?"

"I mean for me. In my front office. Take over the administrative job. You would help me oversee the transactions as they come in and keep a record of the day's business. You can handle a computer, right?"

"Well, sure, my job as a graphics designer was all about translating art to the screen. And I took a couple of courses on keeping accounts. But that was, you know . . . before."

"Our bookkeeping system is designed for folks who argue with numbers. Like me." He realized he was fidgeting and jammed his fingers together across his middle. "The pay is decent and the hours are flexible, so you could take time to see to your little girl. I tried a temp out last week. The young man could not have been dumber if he'd been planted in my front lawn. What do you say?"

Amy realized the man was nervous because he feared she would turn down his offer. And there were any number of reasons why she might be concerned—the run-in with the drug dealers, the unresolved issues with Drew, the cash. But all she could think was, *A real job.* "Mr. Denton— Bob—this is *fantastic.* I would *love* to work there."

"I know you've had a few hard days. But the transactions will be stacked up after this weekend. I need you to start tomorrow."

"Sir, it would be a *pleasure.*" She rose to her feet. "You don't know—You can't possibly have any idea what this means."

He smiled as he rose to his feet and said the same words she had used at their first meeting. "Now's the time you ask me about pay."

— Chapter 14 —

Amy bought Kimmie lunch at the mall food court. She disliked the cavernous din almost as much as Kimmie loved being there. Kimmie had no interest in racing around with the kids or yelling her ya-yas out. Instead, she watched everything. She twisted in her seat as the other kids rushed past. She observed them and the fountains and the shoppers and the sparrows that had slipped inside the mall and lived in the fake trees and stole crumbs. She laid out bits of her fries and managed to tempt one particularly brave bird to within inches of her fingers. Days or weeks from now, Kimmie would mention something she had seen, surprising Amy with what she remembered. Kimmie was the most observant person Amy had ever known.

Which was why, as they walked the mall after lunch, Amy was not entirely surprised when Kimmie asked, "Do you like that man from church?"

"You mean Mr. Denton?"

"He said for you to call him Bob. Should I do that, too?"

"I suppose you can call him Mr. Bob if you want. And yes, I think he's nice. He's honest, and he cares about people."

"He gave you the job. You looked like you were going to cry."

"I was happy."

"He built our home?"

"He helped the church make it."

"So we could live there."

"That's right, honey."

"Are you going to marry him, Mommy?"

"Sweetheart, Bob Denton is my boss. I'm going to work for him." They walked past another couple of stores. "Do you want me to marry someone else, honey? Do you want a new daddy?"

Kimmie gave a huge shrug. "I don't know, Mommy."

Amy nodded. She didn't know, either.

She studied the people as much as the stores. Sundays were a good day for mall walking, because many women dressed in their favorite clothes. Amy saw several outfits she thought would suit her. Then she drove Kimmie to Marshalls. They had done this before when they had money, going first to the mall to study styles, then to Marshalls or T.J. Maxx to find bargains. Amy found Kimmie a pink dress and matching sandals, then a new pair of pink jeans and two matching tops. Amy selected three outfits for herself, two pantsuits and a lovely dress of smoky blue, and three additional blouses, and pumps, and stockings. It was the most she had spent on herself in over two years.

Amy left Marshalls with both hands full of shopping. Kimmie carried her own bag mashed up tight against her chest. As they passed down the line of cars, Amy noticed a man seated behind the wheel of a nondescript gray four-door. With a start, she realized it was Paul Travers. She started to wave, but he turned away, almost as though he didn't see her at all. Amy drove to get groceries, then home, and spent an hour playing dress-up with Kimmie. As she started making Kimmie's favorite dinner, she glanced out the front door. Paul Travers was seated on the sidewalk, watching the empty parking lot.

She left the apartment, walked down the covered sidewalk, and asked, "Don't you ever get bored?"

"If an agent can't be comfortable on surveillance or guard duty, he's not much of an agent."

She nodded. "We're about to have dinner. Want to join us?"

"Better not." He did not look up. "We've got eyes on us."

"The place is empty."

"Because I'm out here. But they're watching." He glanced over. "Thanks just the same."

"You'll be here all night?"

"I'm just making a statement. My teams are on patrol. After dark, they'll swing by every hour to check on things." He pulled a slip of paper from his shirt pocket. "You notice anything, you even *think* there's something odd, you get worried, you call."

She stuffed the paper in her jeans. "How long will you do this?"

"Long as it takes." He met her gaze. "I meant what I said, Amy. You and your daughter are going to be safe."

Paul sat by his apartment's front door as the sun drew late-afternoon shadows over the parking lot. His back was against the former motel's wall, and the soundproofing was shabby enough that he could hear kids inside complaining that they couldn't go outside and play. He knew they were trapped because of his presence. The parents would be fearful over a cop lurking outside their doorway. Having one living in the complex would make them all uncertain. He admired Lucy for giving him the place, because it risked alienating all her other tenants. It was a gift of trust that he intended to repay.

He gave himself over to memories. It was something he rarely did. But the silent lot made for a powerfully reflective mirror. He had joined the FBI straight out of college. Becoming a fed had been his primary goal since high school. He had gone to the University of Maryland because its criminology department was one of the nation's finest, and all federal agencies used it as a recruiting point. During senior year, he had been granted a coveted slot to attend the national police training program at Fort Benning; only sixteen university students were invited. It was considered a launching pad for highfliers.

Paul had graduated from the FBI's training program at the top of his class. He had been sent to headquarters in Washington, expecting great things. For other agents, it would have been a plum assignment. But he had hated the post with a passion. The infighting had astonished him, the petty office politics, the subtle slights, the bruising battles over any hint of advancement. He had managed to survive three years basically by holding his breath. But the strain had cost him dearly. He had married during his last year in college, and his young wife had watched helplessly as he became ever more silent and repressed. Stifling his frustrated rage had left him unable to feel anything at all.

In his fourth year with the feds, he landed a position at the Baltimore office. Baltimore was a sought-after posting, close enough to be noticed by headquarters and a focal point for major crime. But Paul had been on the job less than six months when a raid went bad and he was shot while apprehending a suspect. His wife stuck by him through the hospital and the rehab and the medical discharge. Then she declared she'd had more than enough and left him. Paul had not thought anything could hurt him worse than the bullet, but the divorce had torn him apart. He had turned to his pastor, who offered the strength and solace of a caring man. When the pastor asked his help with another church's moment of crisis, Paul had found a new purpose.

If only his new work were enough to fill the void where his heart once resided.

A deep voice startled him by demanding, "Hey, man, you got a minute?"

Paul jerked out of his reverie as the large black man from the evening session weaved his way through the parked cars. "Absolutely. Can I get you a seat?"

"I'm good. The name's Uriah."

"Like the band?"

"Yeah, only I don't got time for any British white-bread seventies head-banging rock." Uriah leaned against the sidewall. "Look, man, what are you doing here?"

"Helping the church."

"I got that much from Lucy. And it still don't explain nothing." He jerked a thumb behind him. "Does that include helping yourself to the lady down the row?"

Paul met the fierce gaze. "Absolutely not."

"Sure looks that way to me."

"Amy has been threatened by some bad people. I'm here to make sure it doesn't go any further."

Uriah was not convinced. "So how did the lady's problems suddenly become yours?"

"The church has a situation. Amy got mixed up in it by accident. I can't say more than that."

"This church problem got anything to do with that house over by the park? The one where the kids deal off their bikes?"

Paul let the silence hang for a time. "What do you know about that?"

"Enough to stay away. These retired cops been walking the beat around here, that was your idea?"

"Mine and Granville's."

"Granville Burnes is a good man." Uriah's jaw canted slightly to the left when he spoke. Paul suspected it had been broken and poorly set. "Maybe I will sit for a minute or two."

Paul rose and went inside and returned with the other kitchen chair. The black man seated himself and propped his feet on the narrow concrete ledge. Soon after, doors creaked open and children spilled into the afternoon light. Paul said, "Thanks for the stamp of approval."

"These folks, they got a lot of reasons to stay shy around cops."

"Do you live here too?"

"Before. Not anymore. Been in my own place about a year now. I help out some. A lot of us try and give back when we can."

Paul hesitated, then said, "Thanks for helping me out last night. I mean, in the class."

"I know what you mean. I know it's hard for a strong man to ask for help."

"Terrible," Paul agreed.

"Well, I guess I'm done here." Uriah rose to his feet and offered the kids a languid wave. "I hear something about that house, I'll let you know."

"Be careful," Paul warned.

"Man, you don't need to tell me nothing about that."

Monday morning, Amy prepared her daughter's breakfast and dressed for work feeling oddly calm. In a way, the appearance of that woman with her knife had changed everything. The woman had been sent to scare Amy into submission. And she had been halfway successful. Amy was most certainly scared, but she was not submitting. Not to them. No way was she giving up on this place, this home, this job, this church, this new chance at a life for herself and her little girl. Amy's back was to the wall.

Amy dropped Kimmie off at the church's day care, then headed back across the parking lot. Paul fell into step beside her. "Got a minute?"

"I'm headed for work."

"That's why I'm here." He waited for her to unlock the camper's door. "Have you heard about the problem that brought me here in the first place?"

"No."

"Do you want to know?"

She liked how he gave her a chance. As if her vote meant something. She looked at him fully. Paul Travers fit the classic version of handsome, tall and dark and lean and intensely strong. He also carried a hint of danger, a feral scent that surrounded him. She knew some women were drawn to that. She was not one of them. "Do I need to?"

He took his time responding. "There may be a time when it's necessary. I have a feeling that the two issues, yours and the church's, are connected. But I don't have any proof of that."

"Right now I've got all I can handle on my plate."

He nodded. "Granville has a friend on the force. They want you to come by the station and look at some photographs. See if you can identify the people who bought those cars and threatened you."

She felt the tight shiver of invading fear. "Do I have to?"

"No, Amy. He's asking. Not telling." Paul offered a thin smile. "If necessary, I'll remind him of that."

"Then I'm not doing it. I never want to go into another police station as long as I live."

Amy slammed her door. She started the car. Then she sat there. Staring at her white-knuckled grip on the steering wheel. It was one thing to be strong and determined in her little kitchen and another thing entirely to face up to what needed doing.

Paul stood beside her door. Waiting. She rolled down her window. "How would this work?"

"You come back here. Fix your daughter lunch. I'll drive you over, then bring you back."

"You'll stay with me?"

"Every step of the way."

The truck's seat was high enough for her to be right at eye level. She studied Paul's two scars. One was a tight pucker on his neck, below the sharp angle of his jaw. The other was a streak along his right temple. It had clipped off a tiny fragment of his ear. For some reason, the evidence of his past struggles brought her the strength to say, "I'll do it."

"It could help us. A lot."

She nodded and rolled her window up. She put the camper into gear and drove away. Before she had a chance to change her mind.

— Chapter 15 —

The stoplight halted Amy at the main inter-section fronting Denton Chevrolet. The lot was surrounded by fresh bunting that flapped in the hot May breeze. Balloons sprouted from every-where. A mini-dirigible hung directly over the main building, emblazoned with the one word: *Sale*. Her windows gleamed brightly, all part of the festive allure. The light changed, and she drove down another block and parked in her customary spot. She sat there long enough for the heat to gather in the truck's cab. Then she shifted the mirror over so she could look herself in the eye and say, "This is your big chance. Don't mess it up."

Bob Denton was out front talking with a sales-woman Amy recognized. He waved her over, shook her hand, and introduced her to the other woman, whose name Amy was too nervous to remember. Bob took her inside and settled her at the desk outside his office, then rushed out to deal with a customer. Amy sat and endured glances from every direction. She had no idea what to do. Bob was back soon, apologizing and saying that the entire day would be like that. He brought with him a new sales contract and showed her how to enter the data into the system.

Thankfully, she had learned her bookkeeping skills on the same computer program they used. She watched him work through the first two contracts, then she said she thought she could handle it, and he watched as she did the next two herself. The used-car contracts were a bit more complex, as the figures had to be registered against the incoming cost, which often included a trade and some necessary repairs. But by mid-morning she felt comfortable with it all, and Bob clearly agreed, because he left her alone. From time to time she saw him rushing from one group of customers to the next. He stopped by twice more to ask how things were going. A couple of the salespeople came over to introduce themselves, but not many. Just before noon she spotted Drew as he entered the showroom. The young man was nicely groomed, as usual, but no amount of hair gel and flashy clothes could disguise the gray tint to his parchment-taut skin. He kept his sunglasses on in the showroom and pretended not to see her.

Bob Denton chose that moment to walk over and deposit four more sales contracts on her desk. "I know it's your first day and all, but is there any chance you could work late?"

"I think so." It was the opening she had been half wanting and half dreading. "I need to see if someone can watch my daughter. Could I take a little extra time at lunch?"

He was already moving toward another gesticulating salesman. "Sure thing."

Amy drove back and stopped by Kimmie's day care. The after-hours service for working mothers cost a little extra, but it meant Kimmie could bed down in the cubby the children used for their afternoon naps, and she would be watched over by one of the center workers whom she already knew. Amy made the arrangements, then took Kimmie home and made her lunch. The center brought in meals from the church cafeteria, but Amy liked this chance to be alone with her little girl. She fixed herself a peanut butter sandwich but could eat only a few bites. The thought of what was about to happen congealed the food into a cold, hard lump in her gut.

Amy walked Kimmie back to the center and tucked her in to the pallet for her nap. When she returned to the parking lot, Paul was there, waiting by his rental. She did not say anything as she walked over. It would be too easy to change her mind.

The police station was located on the border of Brentonville's original downtown section. Along several side streets, she glimpsed beautiful mock-Victorian homes sheltered beneath live oaks and bougainvilleas. Paul parked outside the station entrance, rose from the car, and walked around to hold her door. She liked how he stood in close, held her arm, shadowed her as they entered the station. Silently letting her know she was not alone, that she could rely on his strength. Which was good, because she wasn't sure her legs could carry her forward.

Amy had never been in a police station before her husband died. Now she had seen the inside of four. Twice she had been stopped on vehicle infractions and twice on vagrancy charges. The last time had been the most humiliating and terrifying. The policewoman had brought in a social worker who'd asked endless questions, tearing holes in the fabric that bound Amy to her little girl. Amy had seen the message in both of those hard gazes, just how close she was to losing her baby.

Granville met them at the door. He must have seen something in Amy's gaze, for he greeted her with "I got your back."

The farther they moved into the station, the more her tension mounted. Blood pounded in her head so loudly that Amy missed hearing the police detective's name. She saw the woman's gold shield and knew it meant she was a detective. Amy knew there was no reason to be this frightened. She knew the real danger was out there on the streets. She knew these people meant to protect her. But her anxiety kept growing until . . .

Paul reached over and gripped her arm. "Why don't we come back another day?"

She saw the goodness in his face and eyes. And the concern. And the strength. It drew her back. Amy took a breath. "No. I'm okay."

"You sure?"

"Yes."

The woman detective started, "I've got a couple of questions I'd like—"

"Later," Paul said, his eyes never leaving Amy's face, "let's walk her through the book and we're gone."

Forty-five minutes later, Paul made them stop. Amy had worked her way through three huge notebooks of mug shots, and the photos were beginning to merge into a single angry face. He drove her back to the church in silence and pulled up next to her camper. "You did good back there."

"I didn't identify any of them."

"There were eight of them in the showroom, right?"

"Three men and five women. Why?"

"You had a good look at all of them, even though only the woman came over and spoke with you?"

"I spent the whole time they were inside painting a window. There was nothing else going on inside the showroom. I saw them." She took a breath. "And they saw me."

Paul nodded. "You heard what I said. Granville, too. We've got your back."

She started to rise from the car but stopped and said what she had been thinking all morning long. "I think we should tell Bob Denton."

Amy liked how he showed her idea respect, how he took time to consider it, though she already knew he disliked it. "I don't know if that's a good plan, Amy."

"He's been very good to me. It's the right thing to do."

"But can he maintain a blank face, knowing his business has been used by the bad guys? We know at least one of his employees isn't clean. Granville claims Denton is good, but can we be sure? You let him in on what's happening, and we need to have answers to all these questions."

"He deserves to know."

Paul was still mulling that over as she rose from the car. She entered her apartment and washed her face and hands, trying to clear away the station's smell and the sullen faces that crowded in behind her eyes. The men and women in the mug shots all wore numbered signs held to their chests. Their rage and the pain still shouted at her. Amy wanted to lie down and close her eyes and let the world slip away for a while. Instead, she got in her camper and drove back to her customary spot down the side road.

When she returned to her desk, she found sixteen sales documents waiting beside her keyboard.

She entered the information into the various systems, noting the charges and the loans and the VINs and all the other details. There was a numbing calmness to the work. It was both complex and yet straightforward. She lost herself in it, such that the next thing she knew, the world beyond her window had gone dark. She eased the cramp in her neck, then phoned the day-care center and spent a few minutes chatting with Kimmie. That was another special feature of Lucy's program, how working mothers were permitted to speak with their children once each day, just have a chance to connect, no matter where they might be.

As she hung up the phone, she saw death enter the showroom.

That was how she thought of it later, when she recalled that moment. One of the men came in, accompanied by two women. Amy recognized them instantly. Drew was nowhere to be seen. But another salesmen rushed over and greeted the man warmly. Clearly, they had done business before. The customer accepted the salesman's fawning greetings like a prince. He was dressed in clothes that must have cost a fortune, a gold and diamond bracelet on one wrist and an oversize gold watch on the other, and a white silk shirt. He was almost too black to be American. His features were very sharply defined. Amy had known some people who looked like that, from the Caribbean islands, folk whose blood maintained a pure tribal strain.

The women moved with a lithe grace, matching his stride, never touching him but very attentive. Then the woman who had confronted Amy spotted her. The woman frowned and instantly turned back to the others. When the salesman stepped away for a moment, she spoke into the man's ear. He stiffened but did not look Amy's way. She kept on with her work, entering the next set of codes and numbers into her system, pretending not to have noticed them. The pile of documents and the computer screen shielded her trembling hands from view.

The man glanced over then, a quick cutaway, his gaze cold, contemptuous. He turned back and murmured something that caused the woman to laugh. She draped her arm over the man's shoulder, dismissing Amy as being of no consequence.

She should have felt relieved. Safety was in remaining invisible. Only not this time.

The man pulsed with a barely suppressed tension. He rocked on his polished boots, heel to toe, heel to toe. He jangled his loose-fitting watch. He flicked his hand like an obsidian whip. He jammed his sunglasses into his shirt pocket, then drew them out and spun them around. Constantly moving, talking, watching.

Amy remained where she was, typing in one set of documents, then another. The drug dealer lounged by the salesman's desk now, up by the main entrance. While all the eyes were elsewhere, Amy lifted her office phone and dialed the number to her cell. Her phone jangled noisily in the quiet room, with its high ceiling and polished floors. Amy answered with a cheery hello, then carried her phone across the room, ignoring the eyes that tracked her.

Once she was outside, she continued over to where the lot's spotlights did not carry. The resulting blackness formed a wall that left her totally invisible to everyone inside. She searched the street, hoping to find Paul. But he wasn't around. She dialed his number from memory. When he answered, she asked, "Where are you?"

"Back at the church. I needed to start the evening crew on their rounds. You need me?"

She watched through the dealership's windows as the group rose from the desk. "No. It's fine."

"You sure?"

As the salesman shook their hands, he laughed at something the man said. In the silent darkness, the salesman looked like a frantic puppet. "Yes. I'm just ready to leave."

"Wait for me. I'll be back at the dealership in ten minutes."

Amy cut the connection and turned on the phone's camera mode. The customers were starting for the exit. She started toward them, holding the phone down by her side. She shot a dozen pictures before the entourage pushed through the glass doors. She passed them with her eyes downcast. They gave no sign that they noticed her at all. Then she walked back inside and slipped the phone into her purse. She could scarcely believe what she had just done.

She was sitting and trying to get her heart rate down when Bob Denton walked through the front doors. "What are you still doing here?"

"I was just finishing up."

He glanced at his watch, shook his head, and said, "Where are you parked?"

"Just down the street."

"Come on, I'll walk you to your car."

"That's not—"

"This area can get rough after dark. From now on, you need to park in the employees' lot."

Bob didn't say anything when she unlocked the camper's door. But Amy knew he did not like the look of her ride. She called Paul on the way home and asked him to stop by. Back at the church, she picked up her little girl and settled her into bed. When she stepped outside her door, Paul was waiting for her. Amy told him, "Three customers came in while you were gone. Two women and a man. It was them."

"You're sure? I don't mean the woman. I'm talking—"

"I know what you meant, and yes, I'm certain. I took pictures."

"Amy, I don't like you taking chances—"

"They didn't see anything." She explained what she had done.

He allowed, "That was smart."

"Thanks."

"No, really. Smart as in a totally professional move." He cradled her phone in both hands. "I'll download these and bring the phone back."

"Leave it till the morning. I'm beat, and my baby's already in bed."

He stopped her from entering the apartment with "Did you tell Bob?"

"Not yet. But I still think we should." She opened her screen door. "Good night, Paul."

He stood there watching as she entered her apartment. Holding the phone. Watching her with respect. She carried that look into her dreams. She had forgotten how good it felt to be strong.

— Chapter 16 —

A thunderstorm swept through sometime after midnight. The first Amy knew about it was when she heard Kimmie's squeals of terror that the big bad truck was coming to eat her. Amy pulled her daughter into her own bed and held her while the lightning shattered their calm. She could hear another child wailing in the apartment beyond the wall. Obviously, her daughter was not the only one wounded by forces beyond their family's control.

The next morning Kimmie woke with sniffles and a fever. Though she was normally a lovely child, whenever Kimmie was unwell, she became clingy and gave in to tears for no reason at all. Amy knew she couldn't take Kimmie to day care, so she phoned Lucy and was given the name of a grandmother four apartments down who looked after other families' children. The Hispanic woman spoke little English but crooned a hello sweet enough to calm Kimmie's fretting. At least long enough for Amy to dress and get out the door.

When Amy emerged from the apartment, Paul was waiting for her. She expected him to object once more about telling Bob Denton. Instead, he told her, "I just got a call from Granville. They have the lab results on your packet. It's cocaine, and it's close to ninety percent pure."

She unlocked her camper and tossed in her purse. "What does that mean?"

"This isn't being trafficked on the street. Ninety percent is the quality you'd find at the level of imports."

"What about my photographs?"

"I sent them over. You were right, by the way. There wasn't a hit from the local books. So we're sending it to allies on the federal level."

There was a great deal she did not understand.

But she did not need to. "I have to be going."

The day sparkled with a freshly scrubbed light as she drove to the dealership. She parked around the corner in her spot and walked past the puddles. The flags fluttered in the weak breeze, and customers were already milling about. The air was humid and growing warmer by the minute. Amy entered the dealership, greeted two passing salespeople, and seated herself at the desk. Her station was a cubby formed by three glass walls. Beyond the windows were two small conference rooms used by the salesmen, separating the floor manager's and Bob Denton's offices. Her desk was positioned directly in front of Bob's door. Six new sales contracts awaited her arrival. She seated herself and got to work.

She studied Bob Denton every time he came into view. She liked how he carried himself, the respect he showed everyone, even those who scorned him behind his back. The work was exacting, but she knew she could do a good job. As the day progressed, she found two entries connected to used car transactions where Bob's former assistant had made errors. Amy hesitated over the first one, but the second one would have resulted in an almost-four-thousand-dollar loss on the sale. So she rose and walked over to where Bob and a saleswoman listened as a couple demanded a further discount. Amy stood where he could see her, and she waited.

Bob gently refused the couple's insistence. They left angry. The saleswoman was clearly disappointed by his decision. He listened to her with the same respect that he had shown the customers. Amy liked the way he handled the emotions and the deal, how he remained firmly resolved and calm in the face of other people's storms. When the saleswoman's heels clicked angrily across the tile floor, Amy walked up and said, "I need to show you something."

He followed her back to the desk, where she walked him through the process. He caught on faster than she expected. "All right. I've seen enough. What does that cost us?"

"Three thousand eight hundred and sixty dollars."

"The accountants might have caught it in their quarterly audit. Then again, they might not have." He leaned in closer to the screen. "Carey is responsible for both this sale and the trade that brought in the vehicle in the first place."

"Yes." Carey was the saleswoman with whom Bob had just quarreled.

"All right. Here's what I want you to do. Let the sale go through."

"But—"

"When this hoopla is done, I want you to come in early or work late, whichever is easier. Go back through all her sales. Let's see, she's been with us for almost two years. Do them all.

It'll require some legwork, because we don't keep our records according to the salesperson."

"I can do that."

"I know you can." He inspected her gravely. "Do I need to ask you to keep this quiet?"

"No."

"I didn't think so." He rose to his feet, looking tired. "Thank you, Amy. This is good work. It's more than that. I've had my suspicions. But I'm not good at accounts. And your predecessor was hired by my father."

When he started to turn away, she decided there would never be a better time. "When you have a moment, there's something else I'd like to speak with you about."

But things picked up midmorning, and they did not have another chance to talk. Lunchtime came and went. Twice Amy phoned and checked on her daughter. The grandmother's English was so poor that Amy finally asked Lucy to go down and have a look. Lucy phoned back to report that Kimmie had slept most of the morning and eaten a good lunch before crawling back into bed.

Amy's lunch consisted of a bag of peanuts from the vending machine and another cup of coffee. Bob Denton was everywhere. He had a sales manager, but he preferred to vet each sale personally before signing off, particularly now, when their high volume and low margins meant a greater risk of error.

Around midafternoon, things quieted down. Bob stood outside the front doors, chatting with a couple of the afternoon crew. Amy went over and stood where he could see her. He jerked slightly, and she realized he had forgotten about her request. "Sorry, in the crush, I completely lost track."

"It's okay. Could I ask you to meet me at my camper in five minutes? It's parked where you walked me last night."

Amy could see the questions in Bob's gaze. But she smiled and turned away, looking for all the world like just another employee having a word with the boss. She didn't know if there was anyone besides Paul who had an eye on her and the company owner. But it seemed best for them to leave the dealership separately. She crossed the north lot, which separated them from the Hyundai/ Subaru dealership next door. This morning she had learned that Bob was co-owner of that company and also held a majority share in the Cadillac dealership down the street. She unlocked the camper, stepped inside, and waited.

Bob knocked on the door, entered, and was startled to find Paul Travers slipping into the camper behind him. Bob asked, "Are you still having problems?"

"Thanks to you folks, things are okay. Please

have a seat." But Paul remained by the door until Granville climbed in.

Bob demanded, "What is going on here?"

"The lady has decided she's going to tell you about an issue we're facing," Granville replied. "I've wanted to do this for days. The local cops insisted I keep quiet. So I'm not saying anything now. But I'm here."

"I don't understand a single word you just spoke," Bob replied.

Amy waited until the four of them were seated at the dinette table and the AC was starting to cool the interior. Bob gave the camper a long look, taking it all in. When he was focused upon her, she started. "Bob, someday I hope I'll be able to tell you what your trust in me has meant. Right now all I can do is tell you what has been happening." She quickly gave him the full version of events, starting with the powder found on Drew's desk alongside the money. And the woman who had tried to warn her off. Paul then chimed in with an overview of how he had come to be here, and the teams patrolling the church perimeter, pushing the boundary of safety ever closer to the house. Granville remained silent, his hands laced across his ample belly, gazing out the side window. When Paul hesitated, Granville spoke for the first time since entering the camper. "Give him the rest."

Bob looked from one to the next. "There's more?"

"The DEA has a house near the church under surveillance," Paul told him. "They have barred the local cops from making an arrest. We've observed kids dealing on the street out front. I tried to take this to friends I still have in Washington, and I was ordered in no uncertain terms to stay out of it."

"That doesn't make sense."

Paul said, "The powder Amy swept off the desk was ninety percent pure. Coke on the street rarely goes above thirty percent. We think there is a link between the house and the coke on Drew's desk."

"I don't follow—" Bob started, and then his eyes widened in horror. "Federal agents suspect I'm involved in drug smuggling?"

"We're fairly certain the feds don't have you on their radar," Paul said.

"We think somebody at your dealership could be," Granville said. "But we don't have any evidence."

"Because of one salesman gone bad?"

"They came back last night," Amy said.

"Who did?"

"One of the men who bought the Corvettes. And two of the women. They didn't work with Drew."

Granville asked, "You did their paperwork?"

"This morning," Amy replied. "A top-of-the-line Camaro. Seventy-two thousand dollars. Cash."

Bob demanded, "Who handled the sale?"

It pained Amy to say, "The woman. Carey."

He sighed. "I'm trapped. Everything I've worked so hard to build up, all the sacrifices . . ."

"Bob, please listen to me." Amy waited for him to lift his gaze. "I've had nineteen months of living with constant fear. I'm trying to put that behind me now. And learning to trust people again is part of this." She took a hard breath. "I trust Paul. And Granville. And you. They say they will keep me safe. I believe them. And I believe they will do the same for you."

Granville smiled across the table at her. "I'm sure somebody somewhere has offered me a nicer compliment. But right now I can't remember who that was."

"I agree," Paul said.

Bob asked them, "What can you do?"

"Whatever it takes," Paul replied.

"It's why I was glad Amy wanted to speak with you," Granville said. "So we could all plan together."

Paul pointed out, "Like I said, we don't think the DEA is aware of this connection. We've spoken with the local police, though. Your assistance could help enormously. If you're willing."

"If I'm willing? Are you serious? Three generations and my family's good name are on the line."

They spent another forty minutes talking things

through. Bob's phone buzzed six times until he finally checked the readout and said, "I've been gone too long."

They shook hands all around and were about to leave when Bob Denton surprised them by saying, "Maybe we should close with a prayer."

Bob Denton set a slow pace on their return to the dealership. Amy was grateful for the time and the silence, as she had found herself deeply impacted by the brief prayer time. Her husband had said often that the best way to judge a man was by listening to the way he prayed. Bob Denton prayed with a blunt simplicity. He was a strong man, yet he was comfortable with humility. He had prayed for his company and for the people and the families who trusted him. He had prayed for clarity, for wisdom, for protection, for strength. He had prayed for Amy and Paul and Granville and the church. About midway through, Amy felt as though her late husband had joined them. Darren seemed to stand in the corner and smile at her, as though everything about this moment was fine in his translucent eyes.

Bob said something as they entered the lot. Amy was so wrapped up in her thoughts that his words did not register. Then she found herself staring at his hand, offering her a set of keys. She glanced over at what stood beside them and said, "You're giving me a car?"

"Of course not, Amy. I'm in the business of *selling* cars. This is a sale. Pure and simple. I'm offering you this Malibu, and I'll take your camper in exchange."

"Bob, you know full well that truck isn't worth the tires it rides on."

He pretended shock. "How on earth do you expect to work at a car company if you can't accept a good deal staring you in the face?"

She studied the vehicle. The silver Malibu gleamed in the light. "It's too much."

"You may have just saved my company."

"All I did was tell you the truth."

"Which they wouldn't have done unless you held their feet to the fire. Don't deny it. I saw it in their faces. Even Granville, who's been my friend for twenty years."

"He wanted to, it's just—"

"They are professionals. They are taught to suspect everybody." He jangled the keys. "One owner, eleven thousand miles, came in yesterday on a trade. Still under warranty."

"I don't know what to say."

"You need this car, Amy. That truck of yours isn't safe. How many miles does it have?"

"Too many. Bob, if you do this deal for a new employee, people will talk."

"Oh, all right. I'll work out a system where we can dock part of the cost from your pay. You drive a hard bargain."

She looked at him, seeing the gentle light in those clear gray eyes. "You're a good friend, Bob."

"Is that a yes?"

She had to wipe her eyes. "Of course it's a yes. This thing is beautiful."

"Well, that's great. Don't know when I've had a harder sell. Now give me the keys to that truck. I'll send over somebody I can afford to lose to drive it back."

— Chapter 17 —

A half hour later, Paul received a call from Granville Burnes. He drove to the church and slipped into Granville's backseat. Consuela Sanchez did not turn around as Paul shut his door and demanded, "Why am I here?"

Granville was already moving. "The feds called Sanchez. They want a meet."

"They asked for us both?"

"They wanted the church security chief," Sanchez replied, "and that's Granville. Then they asked for you by name."

"Which means they know I was asking around," Paul said.

"They most likely flagged our entry into the federal system, asking for information about the photographs Amy shot," Sanchez agreed.

"Did you get anything?"

"Nothing useful," she replied. "Nothing but the call."

They drove in silence and soon entered the high-rise sprawl of downtown Orlando. The federal building was a staid older structure, surrounded on all sides by chrome bastions of newer money and power. It was built with stone quarried from mines north of Tallahassee and offered a smug indifference to the newer structures. As Granville pulled his Mercury into the official lot and flashed his retiree badge, Paul said, "Maybe you should stay out here."

Granville showed genuine surprise. "What, and miss all the fun?"

"Your pension could be at risk," Paul countered. "If they see you as an opponent, they'll come down hard."

"There's not a cop in the state who wouldn't back our play against these guys."

"Our play," Paul repeated, liking the sound of that.

"We're wasting time," Sanchez said.

The Drug Enforcement Agency shared the fourth through the ninth floors with the other federal intelligence groups. This was standard ops in cities where Homeland Security wanted a direct presence yet no single task force required the expense of a secure location. The building entrance had uniformed guards and metal detectors. Upstairs the security was far more thorough.

The fourth-floor sentry was a federal duty officer stationed behind a bulletproof window. The perimeter wall separated the elevators and exits from the offices. As they waited to be logged in, Paul explained the setup—how these top floors were completely isolated, and elevator access was limited to separate machines beyond the safety perimeter. How the space would be split up between the FBI, DEA, labs, federal prosecutors, and other federal agencies.

As Paul spoke, the sentry listened and did not speak. But as he buzzed them through the heavy glass door, the sentry lifted the hand not pressing the button and pretended to adjust his tie. Then he touched the skin beneath his eyes with his two forefingers. Paul gave a tight quarter-nod, just enough to let the man know his signal had registered. The sign was intelligence-speak and came from a series of silent codes used by field operatives. It meant the agent was entering enemy territory. That every person the agent encountered could be the adversary. The threat was real and constant. The operative had to remain constantly on alert. Vigilance was the only way to survive.

A stone-faced woman with an agent's badge dangling from a lanyard around her neck led them down a long hallway and through a pair of double doors bearing the DEA shield. She pointed them to a sofa in the foyer and departed. She did not speak. Paul remained standing. He felt eyes on him from every direction but saw no one. He wanted to be on his feet whenever the adversary appeared. Granville Burnes settled into the sofa and appeared to doze off. Consuela Sanchez inspected the city scene beyond the window. They were comfortable in the manner of partners with years on the shared clock. Paul liked that. A lot.

Finally, the double doors were shoved aside by a man shaped like a battering ram. His head was a polished dome, his mouth a slit as tight as his eyes. He had no neck. His entire body was one straight muscled line, from shoulders to steel-tipped brogans. "Which one of you is Travers?"

Paul replied, "Who's asking?"

"Your executioner. I get half a chance." He jerked his head. "Follow." When Granville lumbered to his feet, the agent said, "Not you."

"We're a team," Paul said. "You want one, you get us all."

The man showed Paul a killer's mirth. "That's not how it goes."

"Actually, it is. And you're not making the rules."

The man burned Paul a moment longer, then turned his gun-barrel gaze toward Consuela. "And you are?"

"Detective Sanchez. I'm here as an official envoy."

"Says who?"

"The Brentonville chief of police."

The agent clearly did not like it but said nothing more as he led them along a back corridor and into the regional director's office. The man behind the desk demanded, "Who's this?"

"Seems the top regional cop wants a witness."

The regional director was a wiry man with slate-gray eyes and a runner's build. "You Travers?"

"Yes."

"Sit."

In response, Paul stepped over to where the agent stood leaning against the wall. Neither Sanchez nor Granville made any move for a chair.

The director sighed. "Why does everything have to be a contest around here?"

Paul crossed his arms. Waited.

"Okay. Beeks, grab a chair."

"I'm good here, Chief."

"I didn't ask what you wanted. Get a chair. You two, sit. Please." When all four were seated across from him, he said, "I'm Ken Grant, special agent in charge. Guy beside you is Special Agent Tom Beeks."

The SAIC showed Paul the same expression he might use with a suspect, letting the criminal simmer in handcuffs, manacled to the metal table in an interview room. The bullish agent seated to Paul's right held an altogether different stance. Tom Beeks did not so much observe him as take aim.

Bring it on, Paul thought, and smiled back across the desk.

The SAIC said, "Mind if I ask why a decorated former federal officer has taken such interest in our area?"

Paul replied, "I was asked to help out with a problem the church is having." He swiveled around to face the squat agent head-on. "You know the church. The one with the school that's under a mile from the drug house you have under surveillance."

The special agent in charge countered, "All federal regulations regarding distance from such potentially questionable activities are being met."

Consuela snorted. "That answer is exactly why I hate working with feds."

"Then let me see if I can make it clear even for you," Beeks snarled. "That place is totally off-limits. You come close, you—"

"All right, enough." Grant kept his voice calm. "We're all on the same side here."

The agent snorted and managed to stomp his feet as he crossed his legs. "I came out of the field for this?"

"Actually, Tom, you came because I ordered you." Ken Grant gave that ten seconds, then turned his attention back to Paul. "We're in the middle of an operation that's cost us hundreds of man-hours. Thousands."

"An operation looking into the transport and distribution of uncut cocaine from Brentonville to other points in the US, am I right?"

The two DEA agents froze. "What do you know about that?"

"I know you're hoping for a break. Which we might be able to offer. But only if you bring in the local force."

Beeks had the bark of a pit bull, a constant rolling growl. "I told you having this meeting would come back and bite you."

"That's right. You did." Grant's voice remained as unchanged as his smile. And as empty. "We have reason to believe that several members of the Brentonville force are on the take."

"That's a lie," Sanchez snapped.

"It's a convenient out," Paul corrected, "used every time the feds want to keep all credit to themselves."

The SAIC gave that another pair of beats, then said, "Tell us how you came into possession of a photograph of our suspect."

"Same response," Paul replied. "Share and share alike."

"Interfering with an ongoing federal investigation will cost you your freedom and this detective here her job. I don't know how to make it any plainer than that." Ken Grant rose to his feet. "Good of you folks to stop by."

— Chapter 18 —

Amy found exquisite delight in the simple act of driving home. She parked in the lot's far corner and rose from the Malibu, hoping her daughter felt better. There was no in-between with Kimmie. She recovered with a child's amazing speed, though, and once well, she didn't want to admit she had ever felt bad.

Kimmie squealed when she saw Amy through the open screen door and danced across the living room to announce, "Juanita is making my dolly a sparkly dress!"

Amy paid the woman and thanked her and then shut the door and let Kimmie show off the new hand-sewn dress and the restored good nature. Once back at their apartment, Amy said, "We're doing something special for dinner."

Kimmie grew still. "But Mommy, we had special yesterday."

"I know. This is another special. My darling girl is all better."

Kimmie remained concerned. "Is it too much money?"

"No, sweetheart." Amy's eyes had been burning quite often recently. "Mommy has a new job, remember?"

"With Mr. Bob."

"That's right." She picked up Kimmie. "Now close your eyes."

"But why?"

"Mommy has a surprise."

"Is it a surprise for me?"

"For both of us. Are they shut?"

"I can't see anything."

"Okay." Amy opened the front door and stepped outside. Kimmie giggled as the screen grazed her shoulder. Amy crossed the lot and said, "Okay, now open."

Kimmie dropped her hands. "What is it, Mommy?"

"What do you see there in front of you?"

"A car."

"*Our* car."

"It's *ours?* Really?" She started squirming. "Let me down!"

Amy did so and opened the rear passenger door to reveal a child's car seat. "How about dinner at a drive-in?"

Kimmie stopped in the process of inspection and looked around. "Where's the camper?"

"I traded it in."

Kimmie's young face was not made for frowns. "But *why,* Mommy?"

"We don't need both, honey." But her daughter's face folded further, and tears started leaking. Amy knelt on the pavement. "Darling, do you miss the truck?"

"Oh, no. I *hated* it. But where will we live?"

"We have our new home, sweetheart."

"What if we have to go back out there again?"

Amy resisted the urge to crush her daughter to her chest. "Mommy is going to do her best to make sure that doesn't happen. Not ever again."

Paul held well back as he followed Amy's new car. He doubted she had noticed him at all as she loaded up her daughter and drove off. There were certain moments in his new work that left him close to tears. Late at night, when his entire world seemed lost and his every day filled with lonely emptiness, he remembered times like this and felt there was genuinely a reason to go on.

After the mother and child had finished dinner and returned to their apartment, Paul phoned Granville. When the voicemail picked up, he called the station and asked for Consuela, but the detective had already left for the day. Paul ate a salad standing at his counter and debated going for a run before the evening session with Lucy's group. He had not exercised properly since his arrival. All this sitting around left him unsettled in his own skin, filled with restless energy. But Paul decided to check on the new shifts, as the daytime teams had expanded their reach by another block. Sooner or later, their encroachment on enemy territory was going to elicit a response. More than likely, that would come at night. Paul decided to walk the loop a couple of times, go to class, meet with Granville, then take a long run before sleep.

The church's small security office was on the opposite side of the gym and cafeteria from the school—close enough to be reached in an emergency, far enough away not to spook the kids. Paul and Granville used the office walls for their maps and team schedules, but it was too small for a gathering. The teams began and ended their shifts in the cafeteria, which made their shift changes less formal and granted the members an opportunity to socialize.

The team members wore the uniform he had suggested—pale blue windbreakers used by the church missions and athletic teams, khaki trousers, navy caps with the church logo stitched in white. Paul wanted his teams to be immediately identifiable, and the caps helped hide their age. He didn't want any local punk seeing the gray hair and thinking these were easy marks. All the teams had experience in either police or armed forces, many in both.

The shift leader told Paul that Granville had canvassed the new neighborhoods, explaining what they were doing and why. Almost everyone appreciated the extra protection and complained about the dark stain spreading from the house on the wide, silent lot just a few blocks away.

Most of the teams treated Paul as a permanent

outsider. They acknowledged him, they accepted his instructions, and that was as far as it went. They might be fellow believers, and he might be there to help the church, but a fed was a fed. He was not one of them.

The team assigned to the new periphery was the most experienced pair, a former police sergeant on the Miami force and a retired MP whose last posting had been the airbase outside Manila. Paul intentionally held back as they exited the building. Two older teams walked their routes around the church buildings, close enough to stop by the facilities whenever they needed. Paul stood by the cafeteria doors and waited until the others disappeared. Then he slipped back inside and stripped off the windbreaker and cap. Underneath he wore black jeans, a navy T-shirt, and black running shoes. He entered the night and pulled a black knit cap from his rear pocket and slipped it on. The men did not expect him to be there, and he wanted to keep his presence hidden.

Just beyond the church parking lot, he slipped off the street and into a vacant lot. He held to the shadows as much as possible while he rushed to catch up. When he spotted the two men, he slowed and kept about fifty yards between them. The former cop and the MP ambled with the easy pace of professionals in no hurry. Their flashlights remained on but pointed straight down. Paul knew the former cop wore his regulation-issue

Smith & Wesson under his windbreaker. The MP preferred a Remington the size of a cannon. Both men still put in serious time at the gun range.

The night was quiet and Paul's mind had ample time to roam. His thoughts returned to Amy and the way she had held her little girl before strapping her into the new child seat. The longer he observed Amy, the more he admired the woman. Paul had seen her obvious terror before entering the police station and respected how she had kept it together and focused on the job at hand. Like most people who had experienced the adrenaline rush of live action, Paul knew the real mark of courage did not come in being unafraid but in not allowing fear to dominate.

He could see why some people, like Lucy, might suspect his motives. Amy was a very attractive lady. She was a long-legged blonde with strong features and a gaze of shattered sapphires. He liked the pale cast to her lips and the light dusting of freckles across her cheeks. He liked the way she treated her little girl most of all. But he did not feel drawn to her in any romantic sense. He couldn't say why that was, and as he raced from one clump of shadows to the next, he felt the hollow ache of suspecting that his ability to love had been stripped away. All he could say for certain was he felt about Amy the same way he would about a sister. He liked her immensely and was determined to keep her safe.

The church steeple was occasionally visible through the canopy of trees and rooftops. The darkening sky was burnt umber, the air humid and thick with various scents. Somewhere close by, a family grilled steaks.

The attack started with the fluid silence of a striking snake. Paul's first warning came when three shadows separated themselves from a vacant lot across the street and glided toward the two men up ahead. One of the assailants clanked as he ran, probably a gun or knife striking a belt buckle. It was enough to spin the two older men around. Paul watched as the MP raised a baton, hiding the motion behind the flashlight that now lit up the approaching trio. The former cop joined his light to that of his mate's and crouched down, taking aim.

The three men were young and slender and overly confident. They spoke with a slurred rush of curses as they moved in, expecting the old guys to fold and flee. Instead, the attacker on the right, the tallest of the trio, was struck by a Taser, cried once, and fell. The two others froze in shock at the sight of their friend in spasms on the pavement. Then the smallest turned back and snarled, "You're going down, man."

He was too slow. The MP had already closed. The baton struck the gun hand and sent the weapon careening off into the night. The youth cried out as the cop stepped in and hammered the third man with a right cross to the neck. All three men were on the ground. The encounter had lasted under twenty seconds.

Paul's attention was elsewhere as the two retired officers knelt by their assailants, flipped them over, and fastened their hands with plastic ties carried by all the team members. The MP had his phone out to call for police backup when the next group surged forward.

This was what Paul had both expected and feared. It was a common street tactic, using newer gang members to test the enemy's strength while the more deadly force waited in the shadows. The two men who emerged from between the houses were bigger and moved with the silent ease of trained killers.

Paul slipped in from the side, moving so quickly and quietly that the first warning either man had was when he flicked open his tactical baton.

The wand preferred by most field agents was titanium and built so that it locked in place; it could be used to stab as well as strike. Most police officers preferred a heavier version they could wield like a baseball bat. But long windups meant a faster assailant could step inside the swing and strike.

Paul had been well-trained. He applied the flexible baton like a metal whip. He moved in and belted the nearest enemy directly across the eyes.

The shock and pain froze the man solid. He probably wasn't even aware that Paul's second strike to his gun hand sent the weapon to the ground.

Paul sensed as much as saw the second man bring up his weapon. He dropped to one knee and rolled. The gunfire blasted a violent light through the night, illuminating Paul as he slipped in close enough to stab the man in the solar plexus, then whip the gun hand, then strike the man's jawline. The man went down hard.

Start to finish, the attack lasted under ten seconds. Paul called softly, "Everybody okay?"

"Thanks to you," the MP replied.

The cop demanded, "Where did you come from?"

"Heaven," the MP replied. "Same place we'd be if it wasn't—"

The soldier's words were chopped off by gunfire slamming out from between the two houses.

The first shot flung the MP over on his back. Then Paul felt something hot and angry hammer him in the shoulder. He spun over, flailing with his good hand, and landed on the serrated grip of one attacker's pistol. He used the prone assailant as a shield and tried to fire back, but the safety latch was on. By the time Paul got it off, the gunman shot again. Then Paul fired, racing through an entire clip in a steady stream, not

151

trying to strike anything so much as hose the dark night.

When the gun clicked empty, he let the weapon fall. Screams resounded from the neighboring houses, and sirens rushed down the street toward them. Paul breathed hard, then heaved himself up and surveyed the scene. The MP was not moving. One of the two men at his feet struggled to rise. Paul stomped down with his heel to the man's neck and said, "You move, you die."

He was still standing there when the first cop car screeched to a halt.

— Chapter 19 —

They gathered for the evening session, twenty-seven of them. Nine were people who resided in the apartments. A couple of others Amy knew by name, including Uriah. Lucy started with a prayer, then turned to one of the men Amy did not know. He started talking about how debt and alcoholism once were his two closest companions. Ten minutes later, Granville rushed in and told them about the shooting.

The group responded with grim swiftness, for clearly this was not the first time they had faced such an event. While the church buildings were cordoned off, Lucy went to calm the children and inform other classes. Granville returned with news that both men were in good condition and offered to drive them to the hospital. Amy arranged for the grandmother to stay with Kimmie. Then they were off, rushing through the night, Lucy talking softly into her phone as they drove. Midway over, she responded to Granville's question by grimly explaining that part of her responsibility was informing the church's senior pastor of any serious incident.

"I guess a shooting of church security might fall into that category," Granville said.

Lucy cradled the phone against her chest with both hands. Passing cars illuminated her grim expression.

Granville demanded, "How is he going to take this news?"

"Our pastor is not the problem," Lucy replied. "If his support of our program could be shaken by such things, we wouldn't exist."

Granville pulled into the hospital lot, turned off the motor, and asked Lucy, "So what's the problem?"

"The elders are split right down the middle," Lucy said. "Half of them wish the church had never gotten involved."

"What, they think the homeless problem is just going to go away? The ladies of the night will pack up on their own? The house will—"

"Yes, Granville. That is exactly what they hope."

When they arrived on the surgical ward, the doctor came out and announced that both men would be fine. Paul's shoulder had apparently been grazed by a ricochet. But the older gentleman was being kept for observation. Amy followed them into the cubicle where Paul was having his shoulder wrapped. His upper torso was punctuated by two other wounds, both of which were well healed, though the scar tissue was enough to leave Amy feeling slightly queasy. Granville spoke a few words of encouragement, then they entered the next room, where an older man was talking to a nurse about Paul saving his life. The former soldier's voice was groggy from pain medication, but he kept telling everyone within reach that Paul Travers was a hero.

Lucy's phone rang, and she carried it back down the hall before answering. Amy watched her stand by the elevators as she spoke. Then Lucy cut the connection, wrapped her arms tightly about her middle, and paced. Granville went over, and when Lucy did not look up, he gently touched her shoulder. Lucy was so lost in her internal struggle that she jerked in surprise. They spoke together for a time, their voices too soft for Amy to hear. Then Granville walked back toward Amy, his expression now matching Lucy's. "Let's give the lady a couple of minutes."

"What's the matter?"

"The church is having its quarterly meeting tomorrow night. The elders have decided to put this issue on the agenda."

"They could stop her work?"

"It's unlikely. But yes. If they wanted, they could shut down her department." Granville watched Lucy pace. "Some of the church members don't much care for her work or the people she invites into their safe little world. The good thing is, Lucy heard about this in time. She'll make sure we have friends there to support us."

Amy watched Granville walk back and offer Lucy a comforting hug. Amy knew that whatever this good woman needed, she would give it without being asked. She had a pretty good idea what that was going to be, and the prospect terrified her. But she was going to do it anyway.

She left the hospital a couple of paces behind them, observing how Granville reached over and touched Lucy's arm, letting her know she was not alone. Amy knew these were her friends. She would stand up for them. And herself. It was time to be heard.

— Chapter 20 —

Amy space-walked through the next day. Not even a glare from Drew worried her. Only when she returned from the office and picked up Kimmie and fixed dinner did the world come into focus. And that was a momentary lapse. Because the closeness of things to come had left her so frightened that she knew she could go forward only if she removed herself as much as possible.

The little apartment complex was eerily quiet at dusk. Amy knew her neighbors felt utterly helpless, so they retreated, like battered turtles, into their shells. That was what carried Amy through her preparations. Because it wasn't just for herself that she was going to act. It wasn't for her daughter. It wasn't for their future. It was for all the silent, frightened people who shared her world.

She arranged for Juanita to babysit, then tucked Kimmie in for the night. The older woman's gaze held the tragic cast of silent resignation. It was exactly what Amy needed, seeing the woman's concern. Amy picked up her Bible and carried it across the parking lot and into the main building. A few people milled around, not many, and no one she recognized. She slipped into the vestibule and walked up the central aisle. A couple of women were in the line of chairs normally reserved for the pastors. They glanced at Amy, then went back to their conversation. Amy settled into the pew and turned to Psalms.

She felt herself resonate with the psalmist's resolve. The quiet determination to hold steadfast to faith and find strength beyond herself had never been clearer. Now that she was here, fear was remarkably absent, as though she had moved beyond all that somehow. She had expected to be swamped in terror; instead, she felt her heart racing, and she saw her hands tremble slightly, and yet it did not touch her.

She prayed, then read, then prayed some more. She found her silent words reaching beyond her own need for a home and a future to all the others who lived there and those who might come later. Gradually, the sanctuary filled. Amy continued to dialogue with God, refusing to allow the rising murmurs or closeness of others to draw her away. She felt someone settle into the seat next to her. When she opened her eyes, she saw it was Bob Denton. The man had his own eyes shut, his big hands clasped over his knees, and she felt closer to him than ever.

Amy continued reading and praying as the pastor called for order. She remained distinctly separate as the gathering ran through the opening church business. She continued it into the initial comments about the teams of people patrolling the neighborhood, and the shooting. She looked up briefly when Granville rose and asked to speak. But she decided she did not need to hear him as much as she needed to hear God, so she returned to her prayers.

The words that drew her back were spoken by one of the women who was there when Amy entered. She was thickset and square-jawed and very determined in the way she demanded, "Well, I for one want to know what business we have bringing this danger into our own backyard!"

The arguments came fast, echoing through the enclave. Amy knew it was time. She bowed her head once more and prayed for wisdom and for strength. She almost left it too long, because when she opened her eyes, she saw Lucy rising from her place across the aisle. Lucy looked over in surprise as Amy stepped forward. Amy said softly, "Let me go first."

The pastor glanced over and saw Lucy drop back into her seat. He looked at Amy and said, "Yes?"

"I live in the apartments. I would like to have a chance to address the group, please."

The woman behind the dais said, "She's not on the agenda."

Bob Denton's voice rose behind her. "She can have my place. Let her speak."

"Very well." The pastor started to step back, then asked, "What is your name?"

"Amy." Up close, the pastor looked buffed and polished yet very genuine. His compassion was as real as his strength. Amy had never spoken with him, yet she found herself liking him. "Amy Dowell."

He repeated her name into the microphone, then backed up and remained standing a few feet from the podium. Amy sensed it was so he could stop her if she said something inappropriate, but she was grateful for his presence. She could feel the intensity and authority radiating from him. She took a long breath. "Two years ago, my husband passed away after a long illness. We didn't have health insurance, and by the time he died, we had lost everything. Our home was gone, our savings, all lost. My daughter was three and a half. We buried our hopes and our futures with that good man. The last time I ever spoke to a crowd was at my Darren's funeral."

The church had gone completely silent; the quiet rustling and whispered conversations were absent. Amy gripped the podium as tightly as she could, trying to keep her hands steady. She had never looked at so many faces before. Not from this angle.

"For the past two years, we've lived from day to day, traveling around the southeast. Before, I was a graphic artist. I found work painting store-front windows. We scraped by. We prayed and we hoped for a better tomorrow. But we had a couple of problems, and the little cash I had put aside was gone, and suddenly, I was one step away from losing my little girl to the system. And if that happened, I knew I wouldn't have the strength to go on."

She knew she was crying because she could no longer see the faces. But her voice remained fairly steady, so a few tears didn't matter. She had shed so many tears. All she knew was, these words needed to be said. By her. Now.

"Then God brought me to this place. God reached down and rescued me and my little girl. He spoke to Lucy Watts. I know this because Lucy told me. We were given a home. We were given a chance. And we were given a great deal more.

"There are two big differences in the ways the church and the government deal with homelessness. A lot of lives depend upon what you're doing, and you need to understand why. First, your program isn't about homelessness. It's about giving people a second chance. And second, your program does a lot more than address the issues that people like me face—the debts, the job, the home. Sure, these things are important. But they're nothing compared to what else you offer. And that is showing us a living faith."

She released her grip long enough to wipe her face because the tears were gathering at the edges of her mouth. Plus, her nose had started running. Two swift swipes, then she went back to clenching the podium.

"That is what I need most of all. To learn how to hope again. To lift up my gaze. I don't have the strength. It's been crushed from me. But you have reminded me that I don't *have* to be strong all the time. All I must do is remember what it means to open my heart to God's gift. To remember what it means to have friends like you—people who love the loveless and offer the beacon of a better tomorrow.

"So that's why I'm up here. To say thank you. Because you have given me a living miracle. And now I have the chance to be the mother my little girl needs."

Amy stopped and turned away. She couldn't see her way back down the carpeted stairs to her seat. She stood uncertainly, trying to clear her eyes, when two figures rushed forward. One of them was Bob Denton; she knew because she could smell his aftershave. The other had his left shoulder and arm strapped in a white bandage. Paul remained by her other side as Bob gripped her and shepherded her down the steps and back into her pew. Then Paul moved away.

Bob kept his arm around her shoulders after they were seated. He did not say anything until Lucy started speaking. Then he whispered, "Well done."

— Chapter 21 —

"One thing you need to know going in," Lucy began, "is that we didn't go looking for a problem."

"Which one are we talking about?" the woman seated behind her said, her voice strident enough to carry to the back of the vestibule. "The drug gang or the homeless?"

"Both. We didn't hunt them down. We simply identified what was in front of us."

"Maybe you should have looked the other way," the woman snapped.

Bob Denton released Amy and rose to his feet. "How does that head-in-the-sand attitude work for the rest of your life?"

The heavyset woman reddened and started to snipe at him, but the pastor lifted his hand. He was still one step removed from the podium. "That's enough. Let Lucy have her say."

Lucy smiled her thanks to the pastor, or tried to. "People involved in prison work talk about the rate of recidivism. This means how many prisoners get out, reoffend, are arrested, and return to the penal system. Those working with homeless people face the same problem. To be successful in my line of work, the first lesson that has to be learned is this: some people want to stay lost.

"My job is to identify those who are looking for a way out. Give them a hand. And show them how to get on with life. A real life. With real hope. And a real tomorrow."

A woman's voice called from the sanctuary, "They terrify me!"

"I understand that. I really do. They represent the downside to life. But, as Amy said, our church offers something you can only find here. Leaving it to the state doesn't work. I know this for a fact. We bring Jesus to our brothers and sisters at the lowest point they will ever know. We offer the eternal light in their darkest hour."

When she was done, the pastor returned to the podium, thanked them all, and said, "Unless anyone else has something to say, let's move on."

Paul lay in his bed and listened to the dawn. The AC in his little apartment made such a racket that it kept him awake, so he turned it on only during the day. A faint breeze puffed out his curtains, bringing in the music of cardinals and mocking-birds and a misguided gull that resided in the vacant lot next door. The fresh air was nice, even when the nighttime temperature did not fall much below the mid-eighties. His shoulder throbbed, and Paul knew it was time to take more pain medication, but he decided to put it off a while longer. Through the wall by his head, he heard music from the next unit. A child began singing in Spanish, and a woman chimed in.

As he rose and brewed coffee, he found himself thinking about the church gathering. He had slipped into the vestibule just as Amy had stepped to the podium. He recalled the surprise on Granville's and Lucy's faces. He heard again Amy's words, and how she had spoken through her own nerves and grief. He remembered how the church had gone still, as though the entire group had obeyed a silent command to pay attention. Then Lucy had arrived at the podium with her own face wet, wearing her tears as a badge of office. Not even wiping her cheeks, just letting the people see the price they all paid in trying to help the helpless.

He filled his mug and took his Bible from the bedside table, where it had lain unopened since he had moved in. He opened to Corinthians, his favorite book, and felt the words resonate through him, sounding in his brain like the voice of an old friend. At the same time, part of him remained attached to the night before. Something had happened during that gathering. He had found himself bonded to the people and the place. He had spent four long years as a professional wanderer, using his skills and his jobs as an excuse to drift. He had remained tied to nothing and no one. Until last night, listening to Amy Dowell speak about new chances and fresh hope.

Paul dressed and emerged from his apartment

to find the special agent in charge of the DEA's Orlando office parked outside his front door. Ken Grant was talking on his phone, but as soon as he spotted Paul, he cut the connection and rose from the car. "How's the shoulder?"

"Twenty-two stitches, three shots, six pills, and the doctors kicked me out the door."

"You need to go in for physical therapy. Make sure the muscles heal so they flex fully."

"Yeah, they sang me that same song." Paul watched as the SAIC leaned back into the car and came out with a pair of coffees. Though he had no desire for another cup, Paul accepted one, knowing it was Grant's peace offering. "Thanks."

Grant had seen Paul hesitate. "I've got sugar and creamer in the car."

"Black is fine."

They took a reflective sip, nodded a joint greeting to two women departing for work, then Ken Grant said, "Your first injury was worse, right?"

"Twelve days in the hospital, four months of rehab. That first time was awful."

"You get hit by the sweats last night?"

"No, surprisingly enough." Paul spotted Granville rounding the apartment's front corner. The burly man saw them and hesitated. Paul waved him over. He went on, "Must have been the pills."

"Every close call I've had, I flash back to the time I caught one." Ken lifted his coffee in greeting to Granville. "That's what finally made me decide to ride a desk."

"They talked to me about that while I was recovering," Paul remembered. "I said no. Much as I wanted to hang on, I knew I'd suffocate."

"The atmosphere does grow stifling at times," Ken agreed. "Not to mention the dread of sending men out where I won't go." He stared into the sunlight. "Or can't."

"It wasn't that. Not for me." Paul was surprised at how easy it was to speak about this, since it had been so hard even to admit to himself. "I spent four years at headquarters before the shooting and always had the feeling of working in somebody else's idea of a good job. I did my best to lie to myself, claiming it was worth it, that I'd grow through this and become a better agent. But all I really did was clamp down on emotions that bubbled up in my private life. When they talked to me about coming back, I knew I couldn't go there. Not even when refusing meant leaving the force. Not even when this was the only job I'd ever been good at."

The more he spoke, the more involved he became with the pavement by his feet. When he finished, Granville said, "You're where you should be, friend."

Paul nodded but did not speak. The word resonated through the hollow space at his core. *Friend.*

Ken Grant cleared his throat. "I'm here in a totally unofficial capacity. But we need to talk."

Paul forced his mind back to the moment. Granville caught his eye and might have winked, a swift flicker, little more than a twitch. "Why don't we step on over here?"

Paul realized what the burly ex-cop had in mind. "Good idea."

Ken sidled down the walk because the two men were headed in that direction. Ten paces on, Granville stopped. Each of the kitchens had a small window, not more than eighteen inches square. The window where Granville leaned was slid open, but the screen and curtain formed a veil over the people inside. From inside the apartment came the sound of a child singing. Paul saw a blond head flit into view, hesitate, then retreat.

Ken Grant demanded, "Why are we standing here?"

"The light," Paul said.

Granville leaned against the wall by the narrow window. "So what's on your mind?"

Ken looked from one to the other, then shrugged and said, "Here's what we know. Up until recently, Florida was home to two major crime syndicates. Miami handled the south and up the east coast. Tampa handled everything else. About ten months ago, we started getting word of a new organization operating out of Orlando. Then it wasn't Orlando, it was nearby, it was here, it was there. Finally, we tracked down a lead. The first hard evidence we had come up with."

"The house," Granville said.

"We have photos of known crime bosses from Denver and Cincinnati making stops there. We have tracked drugs arriving at a small fishing port east of here, passing through, and being sent all over the nation."

Paul could see the rest of the story unfold with tragic finality. "Washington is all over this. And Agent Beeks is desperate to see his name flash in headquarters' high beams."

Ken might have nodded. "Ten days ago, the house went quiet. They're still dealing, but that's it."

"Small-time locals, with the traffic run by kids," Granville said. "Punks and streetwalkers. Exactly what you'd expect from a low-level gang business."

Paul saw where this was headed. "They know you're watching. And Agent Beeks blames us. The church. For blowing his cover."

Ken Grant's features had gone grim. "Always a pleasure, dealing with pros."

"So why are we talking?"

"Because of the photographs," Paul offered. "The ones we shared with Washington. Isn't that right?"

"Those pictures raised alarms at headquarters

like an unignited bomb," Ken confirmed. "I need to know where you got them. And who took them."

Paul and Granville exchanged a long look. Inside the window, a blond head drifted back into view. And remained there. Silent.

Paul replied, "We have a confidential source. She works in a local business. One we trust completely. The source and now the business are helping us in our investigation."

"I need to know who this is," Ken said. "The source and the business."

Paul countered with, "Who was in the photographs?"

"I have been specifically ordered by Washington not to share any information," Grant replied, "about how we received a photograph of a major criminal suspect from a totally different region. One who has never been known to operate in this state before we opened our investigation. And I have already said too much."

"In that case," Granville said, "we've told you all we can."

"Guys, please, this is about to go nuclear."

"Nice doing business with you," Paul said. "And thanks for the coffee."

— Chapter 22 —

Amy took her time leaving the apartment. Kimmie treated the extra attention as a stolen moment. Amy sat on the sofa, braiding Kimmie's hair and reflecting on what she had heard outside her kitchen window. She knew Paul and Granville had held their conversation there so she could listen in safely. She had no idea what to do or how she felt about being secretly involved in their investigation.

Amy found herself returning to the tight sliver of a dream that had awakened her at dawn. The memories were an unwanted tidal wave. The dream had been of her husband—not Darren as he once was, vibrant and full of life and possessing a smile that sparked joy in her heart. This was Darren on his final day, when Amy had looked at him, really looked, and seen beyond the love and the fear and the determination. She had learned to be strong for them both. For almost fifteen months, she had remained by his side, even when he wanted to give up, even when he was ready. Still she had fought. But that day, she had seen the truth. Darren had wasted down to skin and bones. His face had turned craven. Even the hue of his hair had leached away, leaving it the color of dirty glass. She had looked into his eyes and known he was nearly gone. The fight was over. Then he had said it, the words he had spoken any number of times, only she had refused to hear. "You've got to let me go."

This morning Amy sat on the sofa beside her daughter. Kimmie handed her the doll and asked her to braid its hair as well. She watched her hands go through the motions. Darren's words echoed through her all over again. Kimmie took the doll back, and Amy sat staring at the truth there in her empty hands. She was moving on. And part of her was very frightened by that.

After buying gas and some groceries and paying the center for the apartment and power company deposits, she had four thousand eight hundred dollars in her new bank account and another two hundred and forty dollars nestled in her purse. She had not been this flush since hitting the road. Amy cradled her mug and thought of some of the things she had forced herself to ignore for so long. How the road had drummed through the camper's tired suspension, a constant vibration that had left her back numb. How the bald tires had shrilled through the softest of turns. How the slightest nighttime sounds beyond the cracked window by her head always woke her up with a flash of fear. How little things like footsteps on gravel could frighten her. How Kimmie had squealed in terror at every passing truck.

Now the prospect of a future loomed ahead of her. One with new boundaries. Of course she was scared.

The three men outside her window had drifted down closer to the street when Amy emerged. She walked past, giving no sign that she saw the men, paying rapt attention to Kimmie describing a painting she wanted to do in day care. At the center, Lucy waved as they passed and was in the hall waiting when Amy returned from dropping Kimmie off. Lucy greeted her with a fierce hug and the words "What you said last night was pure gold."

"I wanted to help."

"You did more than that. You inspired me. I dreaded standing up there. Always have."

"That makes two of us."

"Sure. I saw that. But you conquered your fear, and it steadied me. Not to mention how a dozen people came up after to tell me how they'd been impacted by your words." Lucy shared a from-the-heart smile. "After the vote, the pastor told me the church needs to go through a gut check every now and then. Hopefully, I'll learn how to follow his lead and take days like that in my stride. Say, in about ten thousand years."

Amy took a deep breath. "Speaking of meeting fears, can I ask you about something else?"

"Anything."

"This morning I got woken up by a dream. I

was back in the hospital with my husband." She related both the dream and the realization that followed. As she spoke, she saw Lucy's tension gradually fade. When she finished, Amy asked, "Does it ever go away?"

Lucy did not need to ask what she was talking about. "We are shaped by the events of our lives. The question you need to be asking is, can you heal to the point where you are in control of your response? Because there will always be events that threaten to strip away your control. Do you understand what I'm saying?"

"I think so." Amy was no longer surprised by the woman's adept manner of reading people. "Why does that scare me?"

"Because the real issue is not whether you lose your fear or your regret or your memories. The real challenge lies in taking control of your *response*. You still have my numbers?"

"Somewhere."

Lucy pulled a card from her pocket and wrote down two numbers. "Home phone and cell. Day or night."

"I don't want to bother you."

"You won't." Lucy patted her shoulder.

Amy pushed back through the doors to the parking lot and wondered what it would be like, to have the ability to focus so totally on others. Giving without measure. Caring even when the whole world invited her to turn away.

Amy left the church building and walked over to where Paul and Granville waited. Sweat patches stained Granville's white shirt. If Paul was affected by the heat, he gave no sign; he said to her, "That was very brave, what you did last night."

"Your words moved me," Granville agreed.

Amy found it difficult to know how to respond. She made do with a small "Thank you."

Granville must have seen her discomfort, for he went on, "Changing the subject, did you hear what was said this morning?"

"Yes, who was that with you in the parking lot?"

"Ken Grant. He runs the local DEA office."

"Are you going to tell him about the dealership?"

"Not unless he helps us. And not unless Bob agrees."

"I need to get to work."

Paul fell into step beside her. "Our contact with the local police force would appreciate it if you'd stop by."

"Not more photos," she protested.

"We're way past mug shots," Granville replied. "The chief wants to meet you."

Amy unlocked her car door. "Should I ask Bob to join us?"

"Good idea." Granville took in her new car and said, "Nice wheels."

Amy drove to the dealership, her thoughts going back repeatedly to the previous night, the morning, the cops, and Lucy most of all. She pulled into the employees' parking area, feeling a very real satisfaction over not needing to hide her vehicle.

The showroom's atmosphere held a palpable edge. Amy noticed it as soon as she pushed through the glass doors. Salespeople glanced her way, then went back to their tight mutterings. This time of day, customers were rare. Mornings were given over to the review of special offers, a recap of the previous day, paperwork, and responses to Internet queries. Today, however, was different. Bob Denton's office door was shut, and the glass partition was covered by the drapes. Amy dropped her purse on her desk, checked through the files in her in-box, and saw that none of the waiting documents were urgent. She followed the saleswoman she was friendliest with into the kitchenette and asked, "What's up around here?"

The woman's name was Rachel, and she was one of the dealership's top performers. Her son had Asperger's, and the job's flexible hours meant she could leave whenever something urgent came up. With Rachel's son, there were a lot of emergencies.

Rachel stirred a packet of Sweet'N Low into a cup of coffee and said, "Nobody's talking. But my money's on Bob Jr."

"He used to work here, right?"

" 'Work' is not the word I would use. Bob Jr. liked to come by, grab his paycheck, drift around." Rachel's eyes cut over to the afternoon crew's empty desks. "Chat with his pals."

Amy felt the chill of sudden urgency. "Drew was his friend?"

"Oh yeah." Rachel took a cautious sip, her eyes agate-hard. "Old Drew and Bob Jr. were best buddies."

"Are they still?"

The hard gaze shifted over. "What exactly are you asking me?"

"Nothing. Nothing at all."

The woman sipped again. "That's probably wise."

Amy returned to her desk and rushed through the eleven sales files that had gathered since her departure the previous afternoon. The day's business gradually accelerated. The sales manager took over in Bob's absence. Amy waited until midmorning to pick up a pair of folders and knock on Bob's door. There was no response. Amy gave it a moment, then opened the door. "Can I speak with you?"

Bob sat in the gloom, his gaze pointed at nothing. "Now's not a good time, Amy."

She entered anyway. Shut the door. Walked over. "Do you want to talk about it?"

He stared at her for a long moment. "Why on

earth would you want to get involved in my mess?"

"That's what friends do, Bob. Help each other through the hard times. Offer strength when it's needed. Like you did for me last night."

He stared at her a long time. "It's my son."

Amy took that as the only invitation she was going to receive and set her folders on the desk and seated herself.

"Bob Jr. is back in rehab. I didn't know anything about it. We haven't spoken in three months. No, four. Last night his counselor phoned. My son has his first family intervention coming up."

"When?"

Lifting his arm seemed to require a genuine effort. "Little over an hour."

"Would you like me to go with you?"

That was apparently enough to bring Bob's day into focus. "You don't know what you're saying."

"Bob, you forget where I've spent the past two years."

He wasn't done. "These encounter sessions are awful. Anything under the sun gets dragged out." He turned his gaze back to the shuttered window. "My son blames me for everything."

"That's pretty standard for somebody in denial. But you've heard that before."

"Hundreds of times. From dozens of therapists." His shoulders jerked in a humorless laugh. "They give me the apologies I've never heard from my son."

Amy rose and returned to her desk. She dropped off the files and slipped her purse onto her shoulder. Then she reentered Bob's office and raised the blinds. She stood in the doorway and said, "Let's go."

He pushed himself from the chair, reached for his jacket, and demanded, "Why are you doing this?"

"Because I'm not letting you go in there alone." She motioned toward the outer door. "I'll drive."

This time, when she crossed the dealership floor, everyone was watching.

— Chapter 23 —

Amy phoned Paul to alert him that she was on the move. But Granville answered, saying that they had switched places. Paul needed to have his dressing changed at the hospital and then would bring the other wounded security guard home. Granville listened as she related what was happening. He said, "Bob Denton deserves better."

"I agree."

"Tell him I'll be praying."

Amy cut the connection and relayed the message. Bob gave no sign that he heard. He neither moved nor spoke during the forty-minute journey, except to give three terse directions— merge onto the Greenway, take the next exit, turn left. Amy drove along a two-lane county road that ran through pastures untouched by Orlando's ever-expanding sprawl. After fifteen miles, to the right rose a wire-mesh fence that would have suited a medium-security prison.

Amy pulled up to the alert guards manning the center's main gates. When Bob made no move, she rolled down her window and gave their names. The guard was buff and calm and professional. He asked for their ID's, checked names on his clipboard, and directed them on.

On the other side of the fence, Bob confessed, "I wasn't going to come. We haven't spoken since I refused to send him more money. He said some terrible things. He's always been able to stab with his words. But somewhere along the way, I lost the ability to defend myself." Bob shifted uncomfortably in his seat. "My wife had a gift for knowing just what needed saying. Somehow the gift got twisted up in Bob Jr."

"I'm so sorry, Bob."

"Thank you." He sighed to his window. "He was such a wonderful kid."

Amy drove along a manicured lawn, skirted the center's private lake, and parked beneath the shade of a massive oleander. "I can come in. Or I can stay out here and pray. Which do you prefer?"

"It's too much to ask."

"Bob, look at me. I'm the woman who has a home and a job because of your good heart. Now tell me what you want."

He stared at the building's front entrance. "I don't want to go in there alone."

"Fine." She reached for his hand. "Let's say a prayer, then we're off."

The building's foyer fronted a broad hall that ran between two counseling rooms. A counselor came out and asked who they were. Bob's voice was reduced to a metallic drone. The counselor turned to her, and Amy replied, "I am Bob's prayer partner."

The counselor was young and bearded and had heard it all. "We limit these sessions to immediate family. No exceptions." He pointed to benches lining the broad hall. "You can wait here."

Seeing Bob's evident unease, she stepped in and hugged him hard. "I'm right here if you need me."

The counseling room's glass partition was so thick that Amy could hear nothing at all. The room's opposite wall held more big windows that framed a manicured lawn and the lake. A number of people wandered the cobblestone paths that meandered around the palms and the flower beds. Inside the counseling room, the visitors sat in padded chairs with their backs to the glass. Amy looked directly at the patients, nine in a loose row. At each end sat a counselor, one male and one female, both holding clipboards. Bob Jr. spent his time joking with the woman seated next to him. Amy thought she recognized the woman from television. Bob Jr. and the woman ignored the counselors as well as the family members seated across from them.

A huge man sauntered down the hall toward her. He must have pushed the scales at four hundred pounds. His legs splayed slightly as he walked, as if the limbs had started to buckle from their load. But his face was friendly and his smile easy. "You family?"

"Just a friend," Amy replied, and pointed at the glass. "I didn't want him to come alone."

"Hey, that's cool. Can be a long hard trip out here on your own." He pointed at the chairs beside hers. "Mind if I take a load off?"

His face was placid and his voice calm. Amy's street radar did not ping. "Go for it."

"Thanks. The name's Hector."

"Nice to meet you, Hector. I'm Amy."

The two chairs groaned as they took his weight. "I don't get my turn in there until this afternoon. The minutes go by slow, waiting. My sister's coming up with my kids. Be good to see them, I guess." He unrolled the sleeve of his T-shirt and extracted a rumpled pack of cigarettes. His upper arm was bigger than Amy's thigh. "Smoke?"

"No, thank you."

He plucked out a cigarette. "So who's your friend's weight?"

She had not heard that term before. But she understood. The *weight*—the burden that held everyone down. "The guy with the lovely smile."

Hector lit up, dragged in a good third of the cigarette, then blew the words "Oh. Him."

"You know Bob Jr.?"

"He's in my counseling session. Goes by BeeJay around here."

Maybe it was the smoke that had flattened Hector's voice, but Amy didn't think so. "I've never met the man, whatever name he uses. And I never want to."

Hector eyed her as he dragged hard. The embers crawled up the cigarette. "You done time, Amy?"

"No. But I lived hard. Two years."

"Then you know."

She glanced back through the glass. "Oh, yeah. I know."

Hector told her anyway. "BeeJay claims he's in because the judge gave him the choice of graduating from rehab or doing hard time."

"He 'claims,' " Amy repeated. When Hector responded with a slow nod, she asked, "Why would you question what he said?"

"Some guys, they just come in for a while. Their habit takes the upper hand, they got to scale back and can't do it on their own. But that's not a cool thing to confess to, you know?" His smile held a sad edge. "Voice of experience and all."

"So this is what happened with BeeJay?"

He dragged on the cigarette, squinting through the glass. "Hard to say. But my gut tells me nothing that comes out of that guy's mouth is the truth."

Amy was thinking hard now. "Is this place expensive?"

"Look around, girl. What do you see?"

"The best of everything."

"Exactly. Me, I got a trust fund. What I don't put up my nose, I spend keeping these places open."

Amy found herself liking the man despite herself. "Sort of like time at the spa."

"There you go." He mashed his cigarette in the ashtray, plucked out another, lit up again. "Why you asking, you want to check in?"

"BeeJay's father isn't paying his tab," Amy replied. "It got me wondering."

His gaze had gone street-hard. "Somebody fronts him the cash for this place, there's bound to be some serious people involved."

"I'm just curious," Amy said.

He heaved himself up and said, "Bad thing, curiosity. Look where it got the poor cat."

— Chapter 24 —

When Bob emerged from the session, Amy greeted him with the same fierce support he had offered the previous night. The counselor thanked Bob for coming, his smile robbing the words of significance. "Your son's formal assessment is in five days. We'll see about setting a release date at that time. Should we contact you then?"

When Bob did not respond, Amy said, "That would be great." She gave the number for Denton Chevrolet. "Come on, Bob."

She kept her arm around him until they reached the car. She waited until he was seated, then shut his door and slipped behind the wheel. She started the car, adjusted the AC, and pulled from the lot. She did not see Granville's car but was not concerned. She assumed he had opted to wait for them beyond the front gates.

When they had passed the security point, she said, "I've been asked to stop by the Brenton-ville police station. If it's too much for you, I could—"

"I don't want to go back to the office."

"That's fine, Bob." She turned onto the main road and looked around but still could not find Granville.

"Amy."

"Yes?"

"Thank you." Bob released his tension with the words. "I needed to do this. I couldn't . . ."

"I understand, Bob."

He continued, "I couldn't do it on my own. I knew what I was going to find in there." He turned his gaze to her. The hollow void was gone, replaced by a sad wisdom. "I needed to say good-bye. I've tried my best to do right by my boy. Now we're done. And I needed a friend's strength to help me close that door."

She slowed enough to study the man. Bob was a remarkable mixture of flexibility and fortitude. He bent, but only so far. His features were strong, yet his gaze held a gentle light even now, when he was so burdened. "You're welcome, Bob. I'm glad I could help."

They passed through an orange grove, and the AC blew the perfume of a million blossoms. Beyond the grove stretched pastureland where cows grazed. Other than a farm truck behind them, the road was empty and glistening in the afternoon heat. The silence was interrupted by the ringing of her phone. She handed Bob her purse. "Will you answer that, please?"

He looked at her. "You'll let me paw through your things?"

She liked having a reason to smile. "I think we've moved beyond sharing a few secrets, don't you?"

He looked at her with an intensity that suggested he wanted to tell her something. She redirected her smile at him. "What?"

He shook his head. "Nothing."

"Answer the phone, Bob."

Bob kept glancing at her as he pulled out her phone and answered. He listened, then said, "Granville is behind us. He says we're being followed."

"Give me the phone, please." She pushed the speaker button, then set it next to the gearshift. "Granville, can you hear me?"

"Black Escalade, tinted windows, hugging the truck's rear bumper. See it?"

It was hard to catch sight, but Amy finally spotted a shadow trailing the farm vehicle. "Yes. Are you sure it's following us?"

"They picked you up as you left the dealership. Waited by the rehab gates until you left. I've asked Consuela to run the plates. Hold on, she's calling."

When the phone went silent, Bob asked, "Who is Consuela?"

"Our contact on the Brentonville police force." She surprised herself with how easily the word emerged. *Our* contact.

The Escalade slipped into the other lane. It looked like a polished tank. Through her closed window, Amy heard the motor roar. The Escalade powered past the truck and launched itself at her. From farther back, Amy heard a horn blow and assumed it was Granville trying to warn her. She didn't need a warning. Amy was as alert as she had ever been.

She mashed the gas pedal to the floor. The Malibu's six cylinders produced a higher pitch than the Escalade, but the car showed a remarkable amount of zip. "Hold on, Bob!"

The Escalade responded with a ferocious bellow and raced to catch up. Bob glanced back and said, "They're gaining!"

Amy's foot was flat against the carpet. She was flying a lot faster than she was comfortable with on a narrow country road. But the Escalade grew ever closer. She heard the pounding beat of the other car's music, like shots that had not yet been fired. As the car pulled up alongside her, Amy risked a glance. She spied a window powering down and a barrel coming into view. "Gun! Gun!"

She did the only thing she could think of, which was to veer hard over, straight into the Escalade. The two cars came together with a mighty crash. Behind her, Granville's horn was blaring full on, and his lights flashed as he raced up. A split second later, Granville slammed into the Escalade's rear.

The attackers might have been expecting Amy to swerve, but Granville's maneuver caught them completely off guard. The shooter's head snapped hard against the chrome window frame. The gun fired, but his aim was off. The shot scarred a noisy groove along Amy's roof.

She shifted her foot off the gas and jammed down hard on the brake. The side of her car shrieked as the two vehicles parted. The Escalade kept moving, shoved forward by Granville. The Chevy's engine roared with rage as it forced the Escalade on, like a silver caboose moving a reluctant engine.

Suddenly, the Escalade burned rubber and peeled off, pulling Granville's bumper partially free as it raced away.

They gathered in the station's bullpen. There wasn't room for all of them to be seated around Consuela's desk, but Amy preferred to stand. She paced a tight circuit, releasing her tension with each step. Paul showed up soon after they did with the wounded MP in tow. Dan Eldridge was a craggy warrior who wielded his crutches with the same impatient disregard that he did his years. Paul and Dan had been returning from the hospital when Granville phoned with the news.

A few minutes later, Consuela ushered them into the office of the police chief, Sandra Burke, a small woman who carried herself with oversize potency. Her features were carved with mannish edges, and her short hair was dyed a metallic copper. She accented her hard blue eyes with matching frames. The woman examined them with arctic intelligence. She ordered Consuela to bring in extra chairs but made no objection when Amy remained standing.

When the introductions were completed, Chief Burke asked the former MP, "Why are you here?"

"Because Paul Travers saved my life." Dan Eldridge looked haggard and in no mood to be pushed around. "I'm looking for a chance to repay the favor."

"As long as that doesn't include taking unnecessary risks," Burke responded.

"I didn't make it this far acting like a green recruit. But whatever comes next, I'm going to be there." He jutted out his jaw, ready for a quarrel.

Burke merely smiled, a thin slice of approval. Then, "Somebody tell me what just went down."

Amy resumed her tight pacing as Granville recounted the events with a pro's terseness. When he was done, the chief demanded, "What do we know about the Escalade?"

"I just got a call from Orlando police," Sanchez replied. "It's been left in airport parking. Stolen plates."

"Did you get a look at your assailants, Ms. Dowell?"

"Just the shooter. He was black. I think there were scars on his cheeks below the sunglasses." Amy shuddered at the flash of the recollected image. "Big. He had to lean down to aim through the window."

The chief did not so much speak as bark, staccato bursts from a blue-eyed pug. "We've got to assume there's a hit out on Ms. Dowell. Which leaves us with three immediate aims. First, protect the lady and her child."

"The church apartment complex has too many access points," Paul said.

Bob spoke for the first time since entering the station. "She can stay with me. I'm in a gated community."

"Which one?"

"Wildwood."

"Top-flight security." The chief nodded. "A number of sports stars live there. That work for you, Ms. Dowell?"

"Is this really necessary? My daughter is just getting settled." The others simply waited, granting her time to see the obvious. "I suppose we have to."

"It would be good to help out," Bob said. "Plus, I've got a whole guest wing just sitting there."

"All right, Bob. Thank you."

The chief nodded and moved on. "Second, we need to determine who the assailants are and why they've targeted Ms. Dowell."

Consuela said, "It all comes back to the house."

"Forget the house," Paul said. He related the

morning's conversation with Ken Grant. "They've moved on. We have to do the same."

"Which leads us to the third point," the chief said. "Who is leading the opposition, and how do we take them down? We need better coordination with the feds. I'll make some calls."

Granville said, "The only connection we've got is the dealership."

"Which means we need to keep Mr. Denton in place and beef up security. Consuela?"

"On it."

Amy said, "Bob had the idea of having me go through old records, seeing if I can find a pattern that might hide money-laundering. Maybe point the finger at certain salespeople."

Bob protested, "I don't want you going back there—"

"I am not sitting this out," Amy declared.

"Mr. Denton has a point," the chief said. "We have to assume there's no longer any subterfuge. They attacked, we defended. They could try again."

The thought chilled Amy, but not enough to hold her back. "This is my church and my friends and my job. *No one* is taking this away from me."

The chief liked that enough to offer another tight smile. "Then we'll just have to keep you safe, won't we?"

Granville said, "Sooner or later, the DEA is going to come down hard, blaming our frontline people for getting in the way, alerting the opposition to their presence."

"Not on my watch, they won't." The chief unlocked a lower drawer and pulled out a pair of shields. "Mr. Denton, Ms. Dowell, do you have any objections to being deputized?"

Amy stared at the shield, amazed at how far she had come, and let Bob answer for them both. "Not if it will help move this forward."

The chief was noting the badge numbers on an official sheet when Granville suggested, "Add another for Paul."

Dan Eldridge cleared his throat. "If you're passing them out, I wouldn't mind having one of my own."

Sandra Burke hesitated only a moment, then slapped another two shields on the desk. "Everybody raise your right hands."

— Chapter 25 —

As Amy left the air-conditioned station, the heat had a cloying impact. The police station's odor seemed strongest out here. Amy could still taste the astringent smell from the unseen cell block.

Bob wanted to take her straight home. Amy had different plans. "I told you inside, I need to go by the dealership."

"It's late, Amy." He hesitated, then added, "I'm tired."

Bob Denton looked more than tired. He looked aged by the day. She explained, "This is a new job and new people. They saw me leave with you. They'll be watching to see what happens next."

Bob nodded slowly. "I guess that makes sense."

"Plus, I need to explain to Kimmie." Amy worried how her daughter was going to take to the idea of pulling up roots again, even if it did mean moving to a big fancy house. "She really likes our little home."

Bob kept nodding. "Does your daughter like dolls?"

"More than anything except maybe peanut butter."

Amy thought she'd held it together pretty well, considering. But when her car came into view, she almost lost it. She had not really seen it when they had arrived at the station. She had been too full of the adrenaline's aftereffects. But as she rounded the corner, a wrecker from Denton Chevrolet was pulling it onto the rear flatbed, drawing the damage up to eye level. "Oh, no."

"Don't worry about it," Bob said.

Jagged streaks were carved down the passenger side, and both windows were cracked. "I haven't even signed the insurance papers."

"I'll take care of it. Granville, will your car make it to the dealership?"

"No problem."

"I'll arrange for a loaner while we straighten the front end. Amy, we'll work something out when this is done. Until then, I doubt you'll be driving yourself."

Amy started to protest, but Bob was already moving for the taxi rank. She let Granville steer her over to his battered vehicle and watched as the wrecker trundled away. "That car was the first nice new thing I've had in a long while."

"Bob is writing off your car as a company expense," Granville replied.

"He's doing what?"

"You drove him out to see his son. Your fast thinking probably saved both your lives." Granville pulled into traffic. "What'd you think he'd do, let you swing in the wind?"

Amy phoned Lucy and briefly recapped what had happened. Lucy was quiet for a time, then asked, "How are you, girl?"

"Okay. Shook up. Kinda beat."

"You sound exhausted. You should rest."

"Later. Right now I need to check in at work. Which means I'll be late picking up my little girl."

"Don't worry about that. Is Paul watching your back?"

"Granville."

"Good. Stay safe, girl."

Amy spent a hard two hours rushing through

the backlog of deals and forms generated by a medium-busy day. She returned a dozen or so calls on Bob's behalf, claiming a personal issue. She said the same thing to the sales manager, who clearly knew enough to respond with a nod. It was only when Amy was packing up to depart when the saleswoman stopped by and asked, "Bob Jr., right?"

"He prefers BeeJay now."

"I really don't care." Rachel eyed Amy over her mug. "Pretty awful, isn't he?"

"I never thought a smile could be that ugly," Amy replied.

"My former best friend from here went out with him. Once. She left for Tulsa soon after."

"He wouldn't even look at his father," Amy said. "Much less talk to him."

"A lot of us appreciate what you did, going with Bob today." Rachel tried to make it a casual question. "What's the connection between you two?"

"Church," Amy replied. "Do you go?"

"A long time ago."

"I don't know how I could have kept it together otherwise. You should come with me."

"I'll think about it." Rachel avoided meeting Amy's eye by sweeping the dealership with her gaze. "I've been here eight years. I've stayed because of Bob. He's honest, he's straight, and he trusts his people to be the same." Her gaze dropped to where Drew leaned against his disorderly desk and talked on the phone. "Maybe he trusts them too much."

Amy fed her daughter an early dinner, spoiled her with a couple of extra Nutter Butter cookies, then sat her down on the sofa and let her play with the new badge. Kimmie traced a finger around the city's emblem and said, "Mommy is a policeman."

"No, honey. I've been deputized. Like Mr. Bob."

"So we're gonna stay with him. At the car place?"

"No, sweetie." Amy had already walked her through this. But Kimmie liked to feel her way around new ideas. Try it from different angles. Taking her time. Amy had learned that impatience was the worst possible response to these repetitive discussions. "We're going to go stay at Mr. Bob's home."

"For how long?"

"I won't know for a while yet. I hope only a few days."

"So you can work for the police."

"That's right. I'm helping Mr. Bob with a problem, and together we're helping the police."

"The police don't scare you anymore?"

Amy hesitated. She tried to be as honest as she could with her daughter. "Yes. I still get frightened sometimes. But not as much."

"They scare me."

"I know."

"They won't take me away?"

Amy swallowed hard. She had not been certain until this very moment that Kimmie had even understood the threat. "No, darling. I won't let them."

The drive to Wildwood took long enough for Kimmie to whine about being sleepy and trapped in the car seat. A nice thing about the camper, one of very few, was how she could tuck her daughter in her bed whenever the little girl was tired. As Kimmie grew increasingly cranky, Amy asked Granville to stop. She shifted to the back-seat, unstrapped her child, and let Kimmie snuggle into her lap. By the time they pulled through the Wildwood security gates, Kimmie was asleep.

Bob Denton's home was a long one-story stucco that stretched the width of his broad lawn. Granville carried their cases and Amy's purse while she scooped up the child and brought her inside. Amy felt infected by Kimmie's weariness. Bob had the door open before they arrived. He smiled a strained welcome and led them through the foyer and across the living room. The house held the grace of a woman's touch, with cream drapes framing the rear deck and pool. The living room had two illuminated display cabinets jammed with the sort of expensive gewgaws that a man would never buy.

The broad plank floor gave way to thick cream carpet by a set of double doors. Bob said softly, "We made this the guest wing. These doors lock."

Granville set the cases inside the hallway and said he'd make sure the police were in place before turning in. When Amy carried her child inside the guest foyer, Bob drew the doors shut behind her. The wing was intensely quiet, as if built to swallow sound. The stubby hall had a door opening on either side and a huge bath at its end. Amy checked the first room and saw a massive bed, the sheets already turned down, so inviting that she felt her exhaustion rise like hunger. She carried Kimmie across the hall to the smaller bedroom and groaned at the sight of a dozen dolls, all of them still in boxes.

Kimmie shifted in her arms and whined, "Sleepy, Mommy."

Amy settled her daughter into the bed, slipped off Kimmie's shoes, and tucked the blanket up to her chin. She stroked her daughter's hair and inspected the dolls. There were four Barbies, a Ken, two Bratz, and a soft Annie. Then she noticed two teddies still bearing tags. She debated whether she should hide them all in the closet, then decided it would do no good. Kimmie would sniff out a new doll like a bloodhound on the scent. Amy dreaded explaining to Bob that it wasn't right. No matter how sweet the invitation was. Because it wasn't about dolls.

Amy kissed her daughter's forehead and whispered, "This has trouble written all over it."

— Chapter 26 —

That evening, Paul was especially strict with the incoming teams. He knew there could have been resistance, especially with Granville not around. But Dan Eldridge settled into a chair next to Paul and kept everyone in line. Dan maintained a frowning vigil that showed the world a single-minded focus on the job at hand. His expression and his silence said that Dan Eldridge did not need to ask questions because he trusted the man in charge. Any potential friction was erased by Dan's steadfast approval.

Paul did not speak to the man until the teams were out on their rounds. "You got your badge?"

"In my back pocket, right next to my gun."

"I want to play shadow again today around the neighborhood. Think maybe you could stay here and supervise the close-in teams, make sure they stay on full alert?"

"Roger that."

"Granville felt it was best not to tell the teams about today's Escalade attack."

"Don't want word to leak out, give the church's

nervous Nellies another reason to fret," Dan agreed.

Paul hesitated, then added, "My gut tells me it's only a matter of time before they try something else."

Dan wore a ferocious scowl. "We'll be ready."

"Phone me if you catch even a hint of trouble." Paul went back to his apartment, slipped into jogging gear, put his holstered pistol and badge and phone in a belt pouch, and went for a run. His shoulder pulsed with each heartbeat, but the ache did not bloom into full-fledged pain; Paul was thrilled to be healing well. He made four circuits of the church, identifying all the teams as he passed, keeping well away from them. He ran by the house twice, from two different directions. The place was utterly unremarkable, one of a thousand single-story homes thrown up in the housing boom of the late sixties. The wide lawn completely isolated the house, the weeds deep enough to almost hide a pair of rusting lawn chairs. On Paul's second circuit, he passed a kid of maybe ten or eleven on a low-rider bike deal a packet of white powder through the side window of a new Lexus. The woman inside turned her face away. The kid pretended not to see him at all.

The evening remained quiet. Paul's only two calls came from Granville, who was spending the day guarding Amy. They had switched positions because the police were now involved in securing the pair and the dealership. They knew and trusted Granville, so his close proximity was vital. Neither Granville nor Paul wanted the cops patrolling the church perimeter. Everything on the surface needed to remain exactly as it had been. Tom Beeks, the DEA agent in charge of monitoring the house, was to be given no reason to erupt. Everything was cool.

Paul went to his apartment and showered and grabbed a bite. He reached the cafeteria just as the last team straggled in. The men and women were aged by the miles they had walked in the Florida heat. They slumped into their seats, rubbed their faces with gym towels, lifted coffee mugs with hands that could not quite hide the tremors. The incoming shift noticed the difference, though a single frown from Dan Eldridge was enough to keep them silent.

Paul returned to his apartment for a rest. It was going to be a long night. When he emerged, he took a casual stroll around the church. The night air was spiced with jacaranda and jasmine and blooming orange trees.

Paul was heading to his car when the old woman who babysat for Amy motioned to him from the apartment parking lot, her stubby fingers curved and compressed by arthritis. As he approached, she called into the apartment, and a younger version of her pushed through the screen door. Juanita's daughter carried a lovely sloe-eyed girl of perhaps three or four. The three waited until he stood before them, then Juanita spoke softly.

Paul knew enough Spanish to understand every third or fourth word. The daughter translated anyway. "My mother, she asks how is the lady, Miss Amy?"

"Safe. We moved her to a different location. For everyone's sake."

"She will return?"

"As soon as this is over."

"And you stay?"

"I need to make sure everyone here is safe as well."

The old woman nestled one hand in the other by her middle. The motion carried a certain formality, as did the way she spoke; her daughter translated, "We are grateful for this gift."

"I'll do all I can to keep you protected."

"My mother, she has something to say. She wants to say it here, you understand?"

"So everyone in the apartments can see."

"It is important that our neighbors understand you are to be trusted."

"What can I do for you?"

"There is a boy. Son of a mother who works long hours. A good boy but a dangerous age. You understand?"

Paul thought of the kid dealing off the bike and replied, "All too well."

The daughter's soft voice carried a stony

202

resilience as she said, "This boy, he was given much money."

Juanita reached into her apron pocket and extracted a tightly rolled sheaf of bills. The roll was held in place by a pair of rubber bands. The outermost bill was a twenty. Paul accepted the money and asked, "Can I talk with him?"

"He is afraid of the police. The family, they have no papers."

"I understand."

"The boy, he wants to be good. He gives the money to his mother. She was in the church when Amy spoke. She wants to help. She says do what you must to keep her boy safe."

"Can the boy describe the one who gave him this money?"

"Tall and very black. African black, you understand? With the marks of a knife on his cheeks."

"I have a photograph I'd like to show him."

"Give me the picture. I will show. It is better."

"All right. Sure. Where did the man meet him?"

"He plays the football, the soccer, with other boys in the lot behind the apartments. A man drove up. Waited. Spoke with him."

"Can he identify the car?"

Even her smile was stony. "He is a ten-year-old boy. Of course he knows the car. It was a Cadillac. The big one."

"An Escalade?"

"That one. Silver-green. New."

"Did he happen to record the license plate?"

"I think not. But I will ask."

"What did the man want?"

The shrug was almost imperceptible. "What they always want. To destroy."

— Chapter 27 —

The next morning started with a ray of sunshine that tickled Amy's face and caused her to sneeze. She opened her eyes to the sound of cardinals and her daughter's singing. The bed was huge and the sheets felt silken. The room was bathed in a glow of comfort and prosperity. The colors were all matched, the dimensions vast, the carpet so soft she never wanted to put on shoes. She slipped into clothes from her case, then walked across the hall to her daughter's room. Her daughter's *room*.

Kimmie was seated in the middle of her own little playground, making tea for a teddy and her ratty old doll and a freshly unwrapped Barbie. All the other dolls and teddies were stacked against the far wall, still in the packaging. Amy leaned in the doorway and wondered at this. She would have expected Kimmie to assault those other boxes with a five-year-old's fervor. Instead, they might as well not have existed.

"Hungry, Mommy."

"Can you say 'Good morning'?"

"Morning, Mommy. Can I have Froot Loops?"

"We'll have to see what Mr. Bob keeps here. Can I have a kiss?"

Kimmie rose and attached the teddy to her side and flounced over. Her expression was serious. As though she was working hard at something internal. Her kiss was perfunctory. Amy asked, "Is something the matter?"

"Hungry."

"*I am* hungry," Amy corrected.

"Froot Loops."

She started to correct her daughter, but Kimmie did not seem to be focused on her at all. Which was very odd. Amy wondered if the child was out of sorts over everything that surrounded her. Or, she amended, everything Kimmie would soon have to give up again. So all she said was "Leave your teddy and let's go find what's for breakfast."

The living room was bathed with a sunrise glow turned molten gold by the diaphanous drapes. The entire rear of the house was a series of floor-to-ceiling doors that opened into an outdoor living area and the swimming pool beyond. Beyond the marble-clad fireplace was a formal dining room with windows on six of its seven sides. Amy had never seen a more beautiful home. But her comments were halted when they entered the open-plan kitchen and she caught sight of what awaited them in the breakfast nook. Or rather, what was there for her daughter.

Three chairs were pulled up to the octagonal table with its inlaid surface. The central chair was piled with a brilliant array of stuffed toys. A giraffe as tall as Kimmie lifted its head above the parrot and bearded elf and pink piglet and elephant and rhino.

Bob was bustling around the kitchen when they entered. He offered a cheery good morning, but Amy caught the hint of nerves. Which meant he was sensitive enough to know he might have overdone things. And that meant the words she needed to say were not going to be totally unexpected. Amy returned his greeting, poured herself a cup of coffee, added milk from a gold-rimmed pitcher, and took a slow look around. She noted the fresh-cut flowers in the crystal vase on the granite countertop, and the array of cereal boxes, and the plate of Danish, and the man watching her with nervous eyes. Then her gaze returned to her daughter. "Come see what you want for breakfast, honey."

"In a minute, Mommy."

"I thought you said you were hungry."

"I am. But this is important."

Amy set down her cup and walked over to where Kimmie stood idly brushing the elf's blue fringe. Her daughter's brow was furrowed with concentration. Up close, Amy saw Kimmie's lips were moving, and she realized the child was counting. "What is it, darling?"

"There aren't enough."

"Sweetheart, what on earth are you talking about?"

"I want everybody to have one."

The realization of what Kimmie had in mind pushed Amy down to a seated position on the floor. "Sweetheart, do you want to give your new dolls to the other children in day care?"

"They're my friends."

Amy started to reach for her child, then pulled her hand back and trapped it in her lap. Nothing could interrupt this exchange, not an embrace, not a tear. She wanted to remember this moment forever. "That's right, darling. They are."

"I bet Gracie's never had a new doll."

"I'm sure that's true for a lot of the little ones in there, honey."

Kimmie stamped the floor with one bare foot. "I don't have enough."

Behind her, Bob cleared his throat. "We could stop by the store on the way in."

All the objections Amy had intended to pass on were lost to the strengthening day. "You hear that, Kimmie? Mr. Bob says we can go get more."

Bob asked, "How many children are there?"

"A lot," Kimmie said solemnly.

Amy slid back a notch, not far, just enough so she could see the man standing by the central counter, the one with the soft eyes, who replied, "Then we'll just have to go get a lot more, won't we?"

Amy helped Kimmie pile the stuffed toys on the floor, then let her decide on the cereal. While she ate a bowl of Frosted Flakes, Amy spread peanut butter over the only type of cracker Bob had, something called stone-ground, which Amy assumed was another word for expensive. She laid some out for Kimmie and had a few herself, then went back to dress for work and prepare Kimmie for the day.

They drove to the toy warehouse, where Bob pushed a massive cart down one aisle after another while Kimmie made a solemn series of choices, buying dolls and stuffed toys for children whose names she did not know.

The toys filled the trunk and half the rear hold of Bob's Tahoe. Amy spotted Granville in a Denton Chevrolet loaner and waved a good morning. Kimmie sang them to the church, as calm and happy as if she had been making this trip for years. As if they were a family.

The only word to describe what happened when they entered the day-care center with load after load of brand-new dolls and toys was *bedlam*. Many of the children cried, their happiness tinged by a pain that lanced Amy's heart wide open. Then she saw the tears on Bob's cheeks and knew that logic played no part in what the morning held. Whatever she needed to say, all would have to wait for a different time.

— Chapter 28 —

The church cafeteria had a small glass-walled atrium that had been fashioned into a café area. The atrium's exterior walls were surrounded by palms and a small but carefully tended garden. Late morning, Paul enjoyed a meal of grilled chicken strips and salad as he related what he had learned from Juanita and her daughter. Granville and Dan Eldridge listened in silence.

"They're pushing," Dan said. "Trying to see how hard they can come on before we push back."

Granville watched a pair of jays strut across the lawn on the glass's other side. "This is about more than just a provocation. They fronted the kid because they want a spotter. A spotter inside means they're after something."

Paul knew it was unprofessional to feel rage at this stage of an investigation. Good agents learned to keep the lid on their emotions. It was the only way to maintain a steady course over the weeks and sometimes months required to reach a successful resolution. But this time he could not help it. "I agree."

"They could have used a local banger to confront the kid," Granville said. His voice sounded metallic, as though clamping down on his own anger turned him robotic. "Instead, it was a major player."

"Big and very black," Paul confirmed. "Accent and knife scars. Driven to the meet. He sits alone in the backseat, two men up front."

"Sounds a lot like the shooter who tried to take out Amy," Granville said. "Shame I didn't get a look at anything except a busted taillight."

"He asked if the kid knew any of the other people living in the apartments," Paul went on. "He asked specifically about the pretty blond lady."

Granville shifted in his seat, as if freeing up the revolver under his jacket, the unconscious response of a cop with thirty years on the beat. "What did the kid tell them?"

"That Amy was gone. She got a job and she left. He didn't know where."

"Good kid." Granville lifted his glass and rattled the ice, a frigid drumbeat. "How are you doing with the teams around here?"

"Fine so far. But they're getting tired. They're old, and the rising heat is taking its toll. Nights require extra vigilance. We need to shorten the shifts."

"We don't have enough personnel."

Paul continued, "And we need to add more teams."

"Same response, doubled," Granville said.

Paul persisted, "A few more days on high alert,

we risk seeing some kind of revolt. Either that or they'll just stop showing up."

"They'll hang in there. I'll see to that," Dan promised. "Okay if I change the subject?"

"Fire away."

"Soon as I heard about the attack yesterday, I knew what was coming next. Escalation."

Paul shared a look with Granville, who said, "I've been thinking the very same thing."

Dan nodded a soldier's tight approval, as if head-butting the sunshine. "The bad guys have an agenda we don't understand. It's pushing them to ignore the downside and take serious risks. They go after a target in broad daylight, riding in a vehicle with plates stolen from another car, you got to figure it's something mighty big."

Anyone who had worked with a major task force knew that organized crime was dominated by two motives—power and money. As long as neither was threatened, the bad guys preferred to go unseen. To draw them out like this meant they felt endangered, and in a significant way. "We're missing something," Paul agreed.

"See, now, that's the federal agent talking. Big-budget task force, all the time in the world to look for motive. We don't have that luxury." Dan's sweeping gesture took in the church around them. "We got people over there counting on us to get rid of this problem and let them go back to sleeping nights."

"Tell us what you're thinking."

Dan gave it to them in quick bursts, the measured fire of a man who knew how to handle an automatic rifle. Three quick taps, pause to re-aim, again.

Paul knew his grin was hungry, and he didn't care. "This is good."

Dan looked from one to the other. "You think?"

"It's better than good," Granville confirmed. "It's what needs doing."

Dan fished out his phone and reached for his crutches. "In that case, I better go wake up a few old friends."

Half an hour later, Dan stowed away his phone and asked Paul to take a ride with him. They did a slow sweep of the church buildings, and then Dan parked in the lot across from the main sanctuary. "I had twenty-eight years on the clock when a rat-tailed punk knifed me in a bar brawl. I spent two years riding a desk, stamped my ticket, and settled down in Brentonville like I belonged. Ellen loves it here. Me, I think it's okay. But there are days, you know what I'm saying? I miss the smell of cordite on the wind. Wouldn't say it to nobody but another old soldier. But there you go."

Paul sat beside the retired MP in his immaculate Jeep Wagoneer. The taciturn warrior tapped the wheel with his heavy gold ring in time to the flow of words. Paul had no idea where the man was going. Or why Dan had asked him to come along on this ride.

"We bought our place on the municipal golf course back in the eighties," Dan went on. "We scrimped and saved so we could have a place that was ours, not tied to the military. Ellen wanted the kids to feel like we had a home waiting for us, even when we rented it out and didn't stay there more than a couple of weeks at the end of every tour. Now the kids want us to sell and move up closer to them. My daughter's a doctor outside Philly, and my son is in IT with an Atlanta firm. Five grandkids. But Ellen and I, we've put down roots here. First time in our lives we can say that. We're just not ready to make another move. May never be, no matter how much we miss watching the grandkids grow up."

Dan's gray Wagoneer was polished to a military sheen. The trees rimming that side of the parking lot offered thick shade. Directly across the six-lane road rose the admin building, the day-care center, and the gym. Farther left was the entrance to the apartment block's parking area. Over to the right was the main school building. Dan had selected his location with a specialist's eye for cover.

Dan scratched the point where the bandage bound his upper left thigh. "I got to tell you, getting shot leaves me feeling every one of my seventy-three years. I can still bench-press my weight, but only twice. It used to be three sets of twenty. I sit over here and take a soldier's nap when I need, three times today. Still, I wouldn't trade this gig for anything in the world. I hate the idle hours, man, deep down I still crave the action. There's nothing so fine as taking down a bad guy."

Paul waited for him to draw breath and asked, "Why are we having this conversation?"

"So I sit over here, put a little distance between me and everything that's going down. And my old brain keeps coming back to the same two things. Do me a favor, will you? One warrior to another. Just think them through. Give it a little time, see how they settle."

"I'm listening."

"What's happening here is some kind of wonderful. You and Lucy and Bob and Granville and Amy, the lady's got some kind of spark, I tell you. We've all become part of something bigger than any one of us." Dan pointed at the corner of the apartment block that could be seen from their vantage point. "The church should walk tall over making all this happen. Not slink around, afraid of what might spring from the next shadow. When you come right down to it, that's our job. Give us the reason and the safety to walk tall."

Paul saw where he was going and said, "I'm just a hired gun."

"See, that's true only if you want it to be. Because the reality is, you've made yourself a home. And I think that's what you need more than anything else right now. Seems to me your heart already knows this. But your mind is still running."

Paul felt the quiet yearning he had spent too long ignoring. He had no idea what to say beyond "I'll think about it."

"Think about this as well. I'm not saying stop your work. Because truth be told, there're a lot of churches out there right now who could use the sort of talents you bring to the table. But why do you insist on doing it alone?"

"I don't see anyone else stepping up."

"Have you asked? Because I got to tell you, there are four or five of us who wouldn't need to think twice before signing on to your next tour of duty. We're not leaders. But we've found ourselves a skipper we're willing to follow. Right into the line of fire."

Paul was still trying to shape a response when his attention was snagged by a glint of sunlight off a car slowly emerging from the side street. "The SUV turning the corner beside the church apartments. Silver-green Escalade."

"I see it." Dan squinted through the sun-splashed windshield. "You sure it's green?"

"It's them. Look, they're slowing. Taking a good look—" Paul felt the adrenaline rush of incoming danger. "The day-care center!"

Dan already had the motor started. He roared, "Hang on!"

Dan's Wagoneer was powered by a six-liter super-charged monster that developed over four hundred horsepower. The Escalade's engine was more powerful, but it carried a ton of extra weight. The four-wheel-drive Wagoneer zoomed from zero to sixty in under six seconds as Dan left his shaded parking space and took the most direct route toward the culprits. He carved a deep furrow through the shrubs that bordered the main parking lot, scraped his way between two imperial palms, and burst through the blooming oleander with such force that he catapulted over the curb and did not even meet the asphalt until he had soared across the first lane and a half.

Whoever sat hidden behind the Escalade's dark-tinted windows must have had their attention focused on the day-care entrance, because they made no attempt to avoid impact until the very last moment. Then the Cadillac's motor roared to life and pulled forward. Not much. But enough.

Dan was powering forward so fast that if he had tried to swerve his car, it would have toppled over. Instead, he tilted the wheel just a fraction, enough to keep the Escalade in his sights but not so much as to lose control. It was a specialist's move, and Paul's adrenaline-amped brain decided the man's heart rate was probably thumping somewhere around forty beats per minute. Calm and cool and totally in control. Even when his face was tight against what must have been some considerable pain from aggravating a fresh wound.

The Escalade jerked forward like a racehorse from the starting gate. Dan's tight maneuver meant they made impact, but not by the nearside doors, as he had intended. Instead, he struck the rear fender.

The collision rammed them both up hard against the seat-belt restraints. Dan released an involuntary groan, and Paul felt his own stitches tear open. The Escalade kept roaring forward, the metal whanging and shrieking. The bolts holding the bumper in place gave way like four gun-shots, and the chrome strip clattered as it hit the pav-ment. The Escalade ran the red light, threaded through traffic, caromed off an air pocket, and disappeared around the corner.

— Chapter 29 —

Amy picked up her little girl and drove back to Bob's house. She went through the motions as she loaded the coffeemaker and turned it on. Her thoughts swirled like heat rising from the deck out back. Paul had phoned her from the hospital where he and Dan had gone to have their wounds checked. He passed over that little tidbit with the casual ease of a man discussing the afternoon thunderstorm. He gave her a brief rundown, cautioning her that they had no idea what precisely the green Escalade was doing on the road in front of the day-care center. His calm was maddening.

The coffeemaker gurgled softly. Kimmie hummed as she played with her ratty doll and the Barbie and the one teddy she had kept for herself. Amy could not stay still. She walked out the front door and down the walk to where the unmarked cop car blocked the drive. The same two stocky men with their regulation crew cuts who had followed her from the dealership to the day care to Bob's home watched her approach. She forced herself to shape a smile and asked if they would like coffee and how they took it. She went back inside and poured their mugs and brought them out and said that Paul and Granville and the others would be arriving soon. The men thanked her and said they'd already been informed. Everything calm and polite and orderly. The road was empty and quiet. The sky overhead was clear and the air cloying with humid heat and tropical blooms. From the distance rumbled a faint threat of another storm.

By the time they all arrived, the day had grown almost black. Thunder rolled and crashed.

Granville and Consuela joked with Paul and Dan over the new dressings, as though there was something funny about the men's return to the hospital. Lucy's mouth crimped tight in disapproval; she clearly felt that their humor was out of place. But Amy did not mind. Their soft chuckles helped keep the lid down tight on her boiling internal state.

Bob brought in extra chairs from somewhere in the back. They gathered in the living room and gave a moment to watching the storm's sudden wrath. Kimmie crawled up into her lap and buried her face in Amy's chest as the lightning grew so close that the blast and the sound came as one. The water fell so hard that it formed a translucent wall off the patio roof.

When the storm passed and Kimmie was back in the dining alcove, playing house, they discussed what had happened. Amy listened to them rehash the events with the terse ease of pros. She had not felt such intense emotions since Darren's illness. Back then, she had forced herself to stifle the worst fears, the metallic rage at the hand life had dealt her. Whether or not God meant all this to happen was a discussion best left for the safety of Sunday school. All she wanted, all she could handle, was surviving the next day, the next hour, the next breath. For Kimmie.

She jerked slightly when she realized that Bob had settled onto the sofa beside her. He handed her a clean handkerchief. For an instant, she did not realize why, until she felt the wet on her cheeks. He looked at her with such grim intent that she thought for a moment he was angry with her. But when she had cleared her eyes, Bob gripped her hand and said, "Nothing is happening to you, your job, or your little girl. You hear what I'm saying?"

Amy found herself so swollen with emotions that she could not speak.

"You are safe here. For as long as you need. No one is touching you or Kimmie. That is *not* happening."

From across the low table, Granville said, "Those people are going down."

Consuela said, "Brentonville's finest are on duty twenty-four-seven. You're safe, and you're going to stay that way."

Amy felt an astonishing bond with this group. Lucy and Granville and Bob and Consuela and Dan and Paul. Her new friends. She managed, "Thank you."

The conversation shifted to what came next. The mood lightened. Dan took a couple of phone calls about some piece of equipment that Paul said was important for the next step, something they were bringing in from Patrick's air base. Amy had no idea what they were talking about, but their quiet strength and determined confidence were immensely reassuring. Bob Denton held her hand and said nothing at all. Amy knew she would probably never be entirely free of everything she carried from the past two years. But here in this moment, surrounded by people who considered her safety worth risking their lives over, holding the hand of a man who had offered her a lifeline, she could honestly draw an easy breath. When the others were busy discussing whatever plan Dan's phone calls had drawn into focus, Amy turned to Bob and said again, "Thank you."

Paul drove back from Bob's home with Granville and Dan. Lucy traveled in Consuela's car. Bob had elected to remain with Amy. Paul was glad for that, both because it kept civilians away from the action and because Amy had looked about half a breath away from coming totally undone. Paul thought about how the two of them had sat on the sofa holding hands. The guy had a good twenty years on her, but what did that matter? They looked solid, as if they fit together. And when they had finished up, as they were getting ready to leave, Bob had suggested they close with prayer. Amy had studied him with a new intensity before bowing her head with the others. Paul liked that, too.

Dan's phone chose that moment to ring. He answered and listened a moment, then shifted around and handed the phone back to where Paul sat alone in the rear seat. "You might as well handle this."

"You sure?"

"Always like to have one voice talking when we're facing action."

"But I'm—"

"You're the lead man," Granville agreed. "Answer the phone."

Paul accepted the phone. "This is Travers."

"This is Sergeant Hawser, out of Patrick's Air Force Base. I'm calling as ordered."

"Roger that. What's your ETA?"

"Sir, this gear isn't what you'd call a record breaker when it comes to speed. It'll take us the better part of a day. Call it fifteen hundred hours tomorrow."

"Want to check your directions with me?"

The sergeant spoke with the laconic professionalism of a guy who had delivered his gear in far worse situations than Brentonville.

Paul confirmed the directions, handed back the phone, then had an idea. "Mind if we stop by the apartments?"

When they pulled in to the apartment parking lot, Paul motioned to the others to stay where they were. He walked down to the apartment holding Juanita's family. The old woman watched his approach through the screen, then turned and spoke into the sheltered interior. Three generations pushed through the door, the little girl nestled into her mother's arms as if this were her favorite place in the whole world. Paul greeted them and asked, "Any chance I could have a word with the boy?"

The middle woman made a weaving motion with the hand not holding her daughter. "It is best if we speak for him."

Paul had been expecting this but had decided there was no reason not to try. "Does he have a way of getting in touch with the bad men?"

"He was given a number to call and a promise of more money."

"All he had to do was tell them where they could find Amy."

"Yes. Is so."

Paul drew a pad and pen from his pocket. He wrote out Bob Denton's address. "Amy is staying here. Ask him to deliver the message tomorrow, late afternoon."

The woman accepted the paper. "You will be waiting?"

"Me and some friends," he confirmed. "Please stress that the timing of the message is important."

"Tomorrow afternoon, I will make clear to him. You will make them go away from here?"

"Far, far away," Paul agreed.

Something of his grim resolve must have emerged with the words, because the woman rewarded him with a broad smile. "The people here with us, they are calling you 'God's warrior.'"

The simple words rocked him in a way he had neither expected nor been prepared for. "I'm just a guy trying to do his best at his job."

"You are a good friend to us." She made the paper disappear. "I will speak to the boy, and he will deliver your message. Go with God, señor."

— Chapter 30 —

The storm had cooled things off, and the sky was luminous. Paul and Consuela sat in Granville's rear seat. All four windows were down. The distant traffic was a constant sibilant hush. The sunlight was diffused through ancient live oaks that lined either side of the road where they waited. It was possible to sit in the quiet car and imagine how this residential area once was. People sitting on their front porches, kids playing games up and down the streets, cars dodging balls and bikes and dogs, neighbors' hands raised in greeting to people they knew and those they didn't. Now the lone car that bounced down the rutted street rattled their car with the bass. The driver gave them the gunner's stare as he passed. Granville and Consuela scoped out the car, then Consuela asked, "Where is your team?"

"Inbound." Paul glanced at his watch. "Five minutes."

Lucy had decided to return to work, which Paul had endorsed instantly. As soon as the backup arrived, this place was going to get very hot indeed.

Consuela demanded, "You trust this to work?"

"Dan was right." Paul stared at the silent house a hundred yards farther down the road and felt the slow-burning anger in his gut. "It's time for a little housecleaning."

Consuela pursed her lips. "I'm only asking on account of how me and the chief have gone out on a limb here. Asking the judge we trust to issue both a writ and a demolition notice. Especially when we couldn't tell him what exactly was going down, since we're still not clear on a lot of this."

Maybe it was the pain meds, or maybe it was just the way Dan Eldridge responded to incoming fire. Whatever the reason, Paul had never sounded more relaxed than now. "You heard the man. When we're done, that problem up there will be gone for good."

Paul heard the faint blaring of horns on the main road and felt more than heard the slow, grinding rumble of the team's approach. "They're here."

The truck made a slow turn onto their street, urged on by a dozen rush-hour car horns. It was not a big vehicle. Nor was it very tall. But it had so many tires on either side that they formed a rolling series of caterpillar-style legs. The flatbed load was covered with a camouflage tarp. The tires scrunched slowly down the street, grinding over the potholes and the gravel.

Dan Eldridge waved them to a halt. The brakes sighed, the massive engine went silent. The doors opened and men in army green climbed down. "Which one is Eldridge?"

"That's me." Dan walked over and shook hands, then waved Paul forward. "This is our lead operative, Paul Travers."

Granville and Consuela joined them. Introductions were made; then together they walked back to stand beside the load. Consuela asked, "What have you got hidden under there?"

"An answer to everybody's prayers," Paul replied. "I hope."

Consuela said, "Just tell me it's not a gun."

"The only explosions will come from inside the house."

"You mean they'll be shooting."

"I expect so."

Dan Eldridge grinned. "I'd hate to think we went to all this trouble for nothing."

The tarp was lashed down in a couple dozen places. Great snakes of bungee-thick cords had to be coiled and set aside before the canvas cover was lifted. The two soldiers enjoyed having an audience and drew back the tarp as if unveiling a prize jewel.

"Whatever it is," Paul said, "it sure is ugly."

"You got that right, sir," the driver agreed. "Don't nobody do ugly like the army."

Consuela said, "Will somebody tell me what it is I'm looking at?"

Dan Eldridge said, "We wanted to call it a Warthog, but the flyboys already had dibs on that. So we had to settle on Road-hog." He patted a dappled green flank. "This sucker will plain flatten anything dumb enough to get in its way."

The massive machine occupying the truck's flatbed was definitely a vehicle of some sort. But there were no front windows, just a tight slit that ran above what looked like a reinforced snowplow. The blade's upper edge was curved down, like a partly unpeeled banana. The plow ran down both sides of the vehicle. There were no doors. Five giant green air vents rose from the truck's rear like stubby camouflaged smokestacks.

The truck driver said, "My orders were to deliver this baby and stand back. Which means one of you folks gets to steer."

Dan pointed at Paul. "That would be you."

Paul saw the others grin and knew nothing would be gained from arguing. Truth be told, he was thrilled by the prospect. "How do I get inside?"

"From the top, sir. Like you was climbing

inside a tank. Which don't stand a chance against my Road-hog, in case you were wondering."

Paul clambered up the side. "Tell me what I'm getting for my nickel."

"The front tires are solid Kevlar and mostly protected by the plow, which is bent down, like you see, to deflect any blast. The half-track band at the back is depleted uranium-reinforced steel. Ditto for the plow and the sides. It was designed to lumber down the road and draw heat from everywhere, so the guys in the rear can stay safe and focus on their targets." The driver was loving this. "Feel like taking her for a spin?"

Paul said, "No time better than now."

Consuela said, "Give me a second." She walked down the empty street, pulled a folded paper from her purse, and tossed it onto the ratty lawn. She walked back and said, "They've just been served."

The entrance was sealed with a submarine-style portal, which the trucker held open while Paul scooted inside. The interior was padded like an asylum cage, and even the control panel was wrapped in foam. The driver leaned through the top and said, "Ain't no sharp edges in this baby, nothing to hurt the driver when you detonate an IED, which the Road-hog was designed to take out." He pointed at the series of buttons in the narrow console. "Push that green button there and light her up."

Paul did as he was told. The entire front and

both sides below the slit windows contained a bank of screens, which all flickered to life. They showed the forward, sides, and rear views with crystal clarity. A screen below the front-and-center view flashed a query: *Start motor y/n?*

The driver said, "Your controls are like a computer game. The stick and them buttons. That's it."

Paul slipped into the chair, which gripped him on all sides like a gentle, padded fist. He clamped the chest belts and fitted his right hand to the control knob. To the left of the control handle was a diamond pattern of buttons, just like an arcade game. He moved the pointer to where it lit up the "yes" and pushed the button on the end of the handle. The motor rumbled to life.

The driver had to shout to be heard. "Okay, you got your reverse and your forward and your idle. How fast do you need to go?"

"Not fast, not far," Paul yelled.

"That's good, because shifting gears in this baby requires a PhD." The driver retreated, shouted something to his mate, then ducked his head back inside. "The ramp's in place. Your reverse cameras are the last ones to your right and your left both. Just draw your handle back toward you a trace—good, that's far enough."

The driver remained where he was, sprawled across the top, while the Road-hog backed slowly and angled as it started down the ramp. Paul thought he could hear the steel groan from the machine's weight. When they leveled off and the two reverse screens showed he was in the center of the street, the driver said, "You're in the green, sir."

Paul waited until the driver had sealed him in, then he pushed the control handle forward. The motor's roar was reduced to a soft growl by the insulation. The air-conditioning was a constant rush. Turning the beast was easy, just angle the lever. Paul started down the road toward his target and nudged the control slightly farther forward. As he accelerated to a slow-walking pace, he passed Granville and Consuela and Dan, who grinned their joyous confusion in reply to Paul's passage. Paul resisted the urge to wave. A couple of dogs emerged from backyards to join the parade. One old woman came out her front door and gaped as he ambled past.

He climbed the curb between two rusting cars and crossed the refuse-strewn front yard. He sat there a few moments, aimed at the enemy, waiting to see if they would come out and surrender.

The house remained blank. Silent.

Paul had no idea who would be inside. But he had no intention of causing bodily harm.

He angled the machine slightly. The half-track jerked a little as it moved. Paul nudged the Road-hog forward. Halted once more, letting the massive beast of a motor do all the warning this crowd should ever need.

He pressed the lever forward. The engine seemed to roar in approval, as though gleeful over the chance to wreak havoc once more.

He peeled the side off the house as easily as taking the skin off ripe fruit. The sound of the grinding destruction was muted to where the engine almost covered the rending wood and screeching metal and scrunching glass. The interior of the house was as dark as a cave. Figures flitted around, and several drew guns and fired. Paul saw the brilliant flashes of gunfire and flinched away, at least at first.

Two men hopped down from the vanished side and aimed at him as he turned slowly around. Only he did not turn cleanly enough, and the plow's tip ground its way through the rear garage's doors. As he took aim at the house once more, he shot a glance through the right rear camera. The garage door lay like an exhausted tongue. Of the new cars, there was no sign.

He peeled another segment of the house off its foundation. The men kept firing from within. There were seven of them now, shouting at him and shooting their guns. Three of them held pistols in each hand, holding them sideways the way characters did in gangster films. Another man appeared in the half-demolished hallway and fired a sawed-off shotgun. The bullets sounded as faint as metal rain.

As he made his second turn in the plowed front

yard, Paul paused long enough to watch Consuela and Granville race over. The former detective moved surprisingly fast for a guy of his size.

Paul hit the lever and started forward, this time aiming for the front door. Just as he felt the steps grind to dust under the plow, the right-hand screen showed the door of the house across the street open up. The two men and one woman clustered on the stoop watched him with a fury that Paul could see despite the distance and the screen's flickering image. One of them was the fireplug of an agent, Tom Beeks. He saw two of them raise phones to their faces.

Paul crashed through the living room and the central hall and the kitchen. He saw mattresses and filthy stacked dishes and smoldering ashtrays and trash everywhere. One room held an array of chemicals and devices used for cooking meth. Then he was through the back door, and the screens cleared of the water shot out of the broken pipes.

Instead of doing another tight turn in the space between the house and the garage, he just kept on going. When he turned back, the Road-hog wore the garage roof like a hat.

Paul took one more crushing run through the house, then continued back across the lawn and left the garage roof in his wake. He trundled over the curb and down the road. The gunfire had stopped, since Consuela and Granville and the

DEA agents had done what they should have been doing from the first day, which was join forces. Gang members were cinched into plastic ties and sprawled on the yard.

Paul drove back to where the two soldiers watched and laughed. The sergeant guided him back up the ramp and secured the Road-hog to the flatbed. Paul cut the motor and climbed down. His ears rang from the sudden silence.

The driver said, "I expect I'll get about four hours down the road and finally come up with what I want to tell you."

His mate spoke for the very first time. "I wouldn't have missed that for Goofy."

"I won't tell anybody what I saw, sir. On account of how nobody would ever believe me."

"Actually, it's on account of how it didn't happen," Paul replied. "And you weren't here."

"Yeah, I believe I heard my lieutenant sing that same song." The driver offered Paul his hand. "I'll be laughing about this for years."

Paul turned and stared behind him. The last portion of the house stood lonely and futile, surrounded by rubble and destruction. A pair of water spouts geysered above where the roof once stood. The gang members were whining and shouting. Paul heard the word "lawyer." A trio of cop cars rushed past them, pulling up over the curb. The DEA agents retreated then, angry and red-faced over having their control stripped away.

Paul said, "Man, that was fun."

"Hey, sir. Next time you need to smash something, the army is just a phone call away. That's the specialty of the Green Machine." The driver motioned to his mate. "Time to vamoose."

— Chapter 31 —

Amy was driven to the supermarket by two crew-cut officers. Bob had looked disappointed over the prospect of having half a dozen others join them for dinner. But the team had just accomplished something important, or so it had sounded in the conversation with Paul. He and Granville and the others were stopping at the station for a bout of paperwork and wrangling with the DEA, then heading over. Amy might be a guest in Bob's house, and she might be extremely aware of the home's undercurrents. But she also knew the power of food.

Kimmie did not particularly like riding in the backseat of a cop car. Her nose wrinkled at the antiseptic smell and she looked uncertainly at her mother when the radio squawked. But the cops both had young children, and they turned down the radio, then did their best to play nice on the ride there and back.

Bob was at the door, awaiting their return. He

helped carry in the groceries and unload the steaks and asparagus and baking potatoes and salad and bread and soft drinks. The officers accepted fresh mugs of coffee, then retreated to their ride. Bob stood tentatively by the kitchen's entry, neither fully in nor out. Finally, Amy said, "Don't hover, Bob. It makes me nervous."

"Sorry, I just . . . Do we want to eat outside on the patio?"

"I think that would be nice, don't you?"

"How many are coming?"

"I have no idea. Quite a few." She couldn't think with the weight of his solemn gaze on her. "Look, would you do me a favor and watch Kimmie while she swims in your pool?"

He brightened. "I've got a couple of inflatable belts the neighbors' kids use."

"Swell. She likes to think she can swim, but you have to watch her."

"I will." But he didn't move. "I want you to be happy. Here. In my house."

Amy set down the knife she had been using to chop the lettuce. Here it came.

"Amy, I fell in love with you the instant you walked into my office."

Even expecting it, she was startled by his directness. "Bob—"

"Everything since then has just given me the reasons for why I want this to work. You and me. Together. How you are with your daughter, how you've held it all together, how you've been since you arrived."

She felt as though she watched herself from a distance. She wiped her hands on a dish towel, then walked over and took Bob's hand. She met his gaze, saw how he was already defeated, fighting his own internal struggle to be open and honest. "Thank you, Bob."

He nodded glumly. "I'm fifty-four years old."

About what she had expected. "I'm thirty-two."

"It's too great a distance between us, that's what you're thinking."

"Actually, it isn't." Close up, the man's craggy strength was clearer still, the light in his gray-blue eyes finely distilled. "I was thinking that what I've been through over the past two years has aged me so fast, the years don't really count anymore."

"Will you tell me about it?"

"Yes, Bob. It's hard, but I will. I probably need to. For myself as well . . ."

"As well as me."

She saw the light in his gaze tighten into a glimmer of hope. And knew she had to set the honest boundary. "Bob, I don't know if I even *can* care for anyone again. Sometimes it feels as though the scar tissue is just too tough."

"Will you try?"

She took one of the hardest breaths of her entire life. "I'm trying now."

Paul felt as though there had been a shift in the house's winds since his last visit. He glanced at the others, wondering if anyone else noticed the change. But Granville and Dan were sharing a joke with Consuela as they stood on the front lawn, waiting for the chief to arrive. The two cops on sentry duty had joined them from the car. On the surface, everything looked pretty normal. Paul walked around the side of the house and saw Kimmie squealing with delight in the pool, while Bob Denton tended coals on the grill and watched her with a gentle intensity.

Paul returned to the front lawn as the chief's car pulled up to the curb.

Bob's neighborhood was old and settled; most of the homes were ranch styles similar to his. But his next-door neighbor had cleared away two lots and built a mega-mansion fronting the lake. The chief saw the direction of Paul's gaze and said, "Home to the Orlando Magic's star center. I went there once for a reception. He's got a pool cage big enough to hold a basketball court. And an aviary."

"Wow."

"Nice guy. He sponsors the local Make-A-Wish foundation and does a walk-around at the children's cancer clinic two or three times each year." Sandra Burke gave Paul a full-voltage glare. "Still doesn't mean I wouldn't arrest him if the need arose. Or you and Granville, for that matter."

"We didn't break any laws, Chief."

"You skirted the edge of half a dozen. Obtaining an order from a hard-nosed judge saved you. This time. You read me?"

"Loud and clear."

The others had gathered behind him; he could feel their presence. But the chief did not budge. "Now tell me why you gave the bad guys Denton's address."

"They're still out there," Granville offered.

"My question still stands."

"We've got officers on twenty-four-hour watch. This development has a solid security detail, and they've been put on alert. Your force is doing hourly drive-bys. We need to find them, arrest them, and get them off the street."

"It's a risk. Our job is to protect our citizens from danger. Not put them in the line of fire."

Granville interrupted, "Heads up, here comes the enemy."

They turned and watched the DEA's special agent in charge rise from his car. Burke snapped, "That is not funny."

Ken Grant walked over. Up close he looked exhausted. "Washington is taking aim. And I'm not sure those deputy badges will protect you from the incoming fire."

Burke stepped between the others and the

newcomer. "My team simply did what your boys should have done the day after you ID'd the house."

"Well, Chief, you are certainly free to have your own opinion." Grant was about to say something more when his gaze latched on something behind him. Paul turned with the others to find Amy standing there, her arms crossed.

She said, "I don't believe we've met."

Paul said, "This is Ken Grant, head of the regional office of the DEA."

Her features pinched up tighter still. "You're the man responsible for letting that house stay in the hands of drug dealers?" Ken Grant waved a vague protest and opened his mouth, but Amy was not done. "I want you to come inside, Agent Grant. I want you to sit down at the table with my little girl, who is five years old and an angel. And I want you to explain to her why it is that federal agents allowed this *scum* to run us from our home and threaten the church that we hold dear."

Ken Grant protested, "I just stopped by to deliver—"

Amy stepped back and pointed at the front door, her features crimped up tight. "*Inside,* mister."

They silently trooped through the home and out onto the patio. Bob Denton shook hands all around and played host while Amy took her daughter in and changed her into dry clothes. They were all seated around the patio table when

Amy returned. She steered her daughter over and said, "Kimmie, this is Agent Grant."

"Why do we have so many police here, Mommy?"

"They're here to keep us safe. Isn't that so, Agent Grant?"

He had the decency to look genuinely ashamed. "Yes, ma'am. It is."

Sandra Burke greeted the child with solemn formality. Kimmie liked that enough to ask to be seated next to the police chief. The small woman and the golden-haired child gave each other a grave inspection. Burke must have arrived at some internal decision, because she said, "You strike me as a very brave young lady."

"I've been scared. A lot. But not now."

"I'm glad."

"Mommy has good friends here. They want us to be safe. Isn't that right?"

"It sure is." Amy blistered Ken Grant with a single look. "Sweetie, ask Chief Burke if she would cut up your meat."

"It's Sandra, and it would be a pleasure."

Amy drifted back and forth from the grill to the table until everyone was served. When she and Bob finally took their seats, he said, "Why don't I lead us in prayer?"

Paul was slow lowering his head. He liked how Amy's hand fit comfortably into Bob's. He liked how Sandra Burke said *Amen,* how she asked about the church and the apartments. How the chief softened every time she looked at the child seated next to her. They ate mostly in silence, a few compliments passed up to the hosts, a few murmurs about how the day had cooled to a pleasant temperature. The atmosphere was not entirely easy, but there was a truce in the group, held in place by Amy's quiet intensity. Paul hid his smile, though he was very pleased by how the woman had risen to the occasion. He caught Granville's gaze across the table. The big man's eyes tightened in shared secret mirth. Clearly, he thought the same. Paul was uncertain about a great deal in his life. But he was almost positive this woman and her little girl were going to make it just fine.

Paul followed Amy's gaze to Bob. The gentleman had sunk inside himself. Amy said softly, "What's the matter, Bob?"

Bob gave a teenager's shrug. "Oh, nothing."

"Don't be like that. What is it?"

"I was thinking about my son."

She grimaced, and she reached out, and she folded his hand into hers.

Bob stared at the table. "The last time I had so many people over here, I'd come back from a trip to Detroit a couple of days early. Bob Jr. had broken in to the house. There were people everywhere. Six o'clock in the morning and they were still partying. There were drugs. I don't know drugs, but I know people, and I know they don't laugh like that or act like that unless . . ."

Amy took a stronger hold on his hand, a comforting light to her features.

Bob went on, "I told everybody to get out. They just laughed. I never felt so out of place, and here I was in my own house. I picked up the phone. I was calling 911 when this man reached out and told me to put it down. I didn't even see the gun at first. Only how the woman he was with kept laughing at me. And my son was there in the background, grinning like it was all a great show."

Amy leaned back in her seat so fast and hard that Paul had the distinct impression that an invisible fist had rammed into her. She stared down the table, her eyes on fire.

Bob did not notice. "I left the house and drove to the office. Stayed there all day. Asked Granville to come back with me."

"The place was a wreck," Granville said softly. "But empty."

Paul seemed to be the only one to notice how Amy nodded to herself, with dark strength in her features as she stared at the table.

"Three weeks later, Bob Jr. called and asked me for a loan. I refused. We argued. He said some terrible things. I hung up on him. We didn't speak again until I showed up at the rehab center."

The cicadas hummed their feverish beat. A

hunting bird gave a piercing cry. Otherwise the night was quiet. Until Amy said, "It's not me they're after."

Paul was the first to respond, because he had been half expecting something big. "Explain."

She kept nodding slowly. "A green Escalade. That's what you said."

"Silver-green," Dan Eldridge corrected. "Missing a rear bumper."

Paul said, "Amy, where are you going with this?"

She turned to Bob. Spoke with a quiet gravity. "Something you said on the drive back from the rehab center. I should have thought of this before. But they attacked, and then it's been one thing after another."

Bob must have read the news in her face, for he did not ask. He declared, "You think my son is involved."

The DEA agent cleared his throat. "Sorry, I'm not following."

Amy swiveled her head around with the slow deliberation of a tank turret taking aim. "That's hardly any concern of ours, is it? Unless we're all friends here at the table."

"I—"

Granville took that up. "You've got a choice to make. You can take your leave. And go back to your games. Or you can join us. Be part of *our* team."

"Treat us like allies," Paul agreed.

"From this moment forward," Granville said, "it's your call."

Ken Grant took his time. Paul liked him for that. He drained his glass of Coke, rattled the ice, and said, "This could cost me my post. But I agree."

Sandra Burke revealed a truly beautiful smile. "Better late than never."

Paul asked Amy, "Will you explain what you've been thinking?"

Amy scooped up Kimmie, stroked the golden head, and said, "As soon as I've put the little one down, I'll tell you everything."

Most senior agents Paul had known and worked with were experts at the process called grandstanding, where everything that threatened their superiority was treated as an excuse to fight for the upper hand. Ken Grant proved to be an exception to that rule, for he opened his mouth only to ask for clarification of a few matters. By the time they'd cleared the table and Bob had made coffee and Consuela had carried out a tray of mugs, they were describing the attack after Bob and Amy visited the rehab center and the connection to the kid at the apartment block and the sighting of the same Escalade outside the day-care center.

Ken Grant took his coffee and paced between the table and the pool. He asked them to go back over a couple of the points. He was still rehashing when Amy resumed her seat. The others were content to wait while he decided. "Tom Beeks has been taking aim in the wrong direction."

"No argument here," Granville said.

Grant ran a hand through what hair he had left. "What a total, utter mess."

Paul said, "Tell us about the man in the photographs we sent you."

Ken Grant slipped into the chair, stretched out his legs, and said, "His name is Lionel Abdul. He basically runs Cincinnati. His mother is Nigerian, his father unknown. The mother refused to put a name down in the birth records. He did the hash-mark scars on his own cheeks while he was inside. He's never done business in Florida before."

Sandra Burke drew out a pen and pad. "But you've known he's been involved with the house."

"Oh yeah. We knew." Grant met the chief's gaze. "As of this moment, my career is in your hands."

"Noted." Sandra turned to Amy. "Mind telling me what was behind your earlier comment?"

"Paul said the car that shot at us was stolen from the Cadillac dealership. Off the truck. Before an alarm could be fitted." Amy asked Bob, "Your son worked at the dealership, didn't he?"

"I wouldn't call it work."

She persisted. "You placed him there because he is part owner of that dealership, isn't that right?"

The chief and the federal agent shared an indrawn breath.

Amy went on, "So Bob Jr. spends a few months grabbing a paycheck, wandering around the dealerships, making pals with guys who share his enjoyment of a good time."

"Building his network," Paul said.

Amy nodded, but her gaze was locked on Bob as if she were willing him to be strong. "Your son, he stands to inherit, doesn't he?"

Bob's voice cracked. "He's all I had in the world."

"So your son invites you out for the family encounter session. He doesn't even bother talking with you while you're there. You leave, and we're attacked."

"And he's got a perfect alibi," Paul said.

Sandra Burke rose. "I need to ensure he does not leave there."

Ken Grant asked, "Can my agents tag along?"

The chief paused in the process of dialing. "We're on the same team, right, Ken?"

"From this moment on."

"Then absolutely. Always glad to have Washington's assistance."

The exchange was lost on Amy, who had reached forward and drawn Bob's head down to her shoulder. She stroked his gray hair and whispered softly into the man's ear, "I'm so sorry." Paul was too far away to actually hear the words. But he felt their impact. And counted the night as good.

— Chapter 32 —

Amy awoke with the gasping shock that had punctuated too many of her nights on the road. Anything could set her off back then—a car horn, the scrunch of gravel under boots, a slamming door, a whimper from beyond the night. Now it was usually a nightmare. They were quick things, seldom much longer than a gunshot. Tonight it was a dream that lasted only a few seconds, just the long streak of taillights seen through a rainy windshield, the wipers flapping hard and doing little good, then the blare of a horn and slamming brakes, and she knew she wouldn't be able to stop in time. That was all. But it was enough to draw up the old horrors, the closeness to losing control. All there. Inside. Waiting.

Bob Denton's guest room held an artificial silence. The carpet and the drapes swallowed sound. But these did not make up a home she could count on. No matter what Bob might say.

She slipped into a T-shirt and shorts and opened the door leading to the living room. Then she went back inside and picked up her Bible. She checked on Kimmie and saw that she was sleeping comfortably. Amy walked through the living room and slid open the patio doors. The pool lights were on, and insects buzzed against the screens. It was a beautiful setting, with the lake a dark, glistening surface that stretched out beyond the lawn. But all this was Bob's. And she couldn't claim it just because he offered it. To do so would make a falsehood of everything she had fought so hard to hold on to. The goodness, the simple rightness, of being who she was.

The door slid open behind her. Bob asked softly, "Mind a little company?"

She found herself glad he was there. And gladder still to find him carrying his Book. She liked the worn surface, the way the leather cover fitted to his hand. The reading glasses in his other hand suggested this was both a natural and regular part of his nights.

He accepted her silence with the ease of an old friend. He pulled a chair next to hers and settled the Book in his lap. "I don't come out here for answers. A lot of the time, I'm not even able to ask for comfort. But sometimes I go back to bed having found both."

"Or they've found you."

"Something like that."

"Would you read me something, Bob?"

"Gladly." He opened to Psalms. Amy listened

and felt her heart grow calm. When he'd worked his way through two, he went quiet. She said, "I had a bad dream."

"Do you want to talk about it?"

"It seems far away now, thanks to you. I'd like to keep it that way."

"Fine."

Later, when she was back under the covers in her too-quiet room, it seemed to Amy that they had been awakened for that very purpose. So they could sit there together and enjoy a moment's peace. So she could gather herself for the next challenge. The ringing cell phone.

The sound amped her heart rate to overdrive. She did not so much move to the phone as fly. "Yes?"

Paul said, "They're coming."

— Chapter 33 —

Kimmie did not like being woken up, not even a little bit. She was cranky enough to fight against Amy trying to dress her. "I don't *want* to move again!"

"I know, sweetie. I know."

"I want to go *home!*"

"So do I, darling. Raise your other arm."

"No, Mommy! Let me go to *bed!*"

"Darling, we have to do this."

"But *why*, Mommy? Is it the big bad truck?"

"No. Well, sort of."

"You said you'd *protect* me."

Amy was not going to lose it. She was not going to snap at her child. But she did give up on trying to dress her. Amy swept Kimmie up in her arms and draped the blouse over her bare shoulders. "That's what I'm doing, honey. As hard as I possibly can."

Bob chose that moment to appear in the doorway. "We're ready."

"So are we."

"No, Mommy! I don't want to!"

"I know, Kimmie." Amy followed Bob at something just under a trot as Paul and Granville stood by the rear doors, both men in fully amped mode. She spared a moment's astonishment over how they could live for this, day after day. They shone with a professional readiness to run toward whatever danger this particular night held.

Kimmie hated it all. She did not whimper and she did not quite wail but settled on a keening note that somehow combined the two. Amy rushed behind Bob across the side lawn, through the hedge, and up to the biggest home she had ever seen. The bouncing rhythm punctuated Kimmie's plaintive cry.

The man standing in the doorway matched the house. He was huge. Everything about him was oversize, including the smile. At two in the morning. "Well, hey there, baby doll. What's the word?" he said to Kimmie.

Kimmie's complaint cut off cleanly. She peered at the man and his grin through the veil of her hair. "I don't want to be here."

"Yeah, baby girl, I get that a lot." He pushed the door open wider. "But everybody's got to be somewhere, right?"

Amy said, "I'm Amy, and I'm so sorry."

"Kareem. And don't worry about it. Hey, Bob."

"Thanks so much, Kareem."

"No sweat, man. The cops got you covered?"

Paul said, "We do."

They remained in the open doorway until they saw Paul and Granville disappear inside Bob's home. Kareem asked, "They gonna play bait for the bad guys?"

"Something like that."

Kimmie said, "Let me down, Mommy."

Amy set down her child and held her hand as she gawked at the enormous front hall, the three-tiered balcony running around the central living area, and the pool cage. Which was illuminated by arc lights and held an Olympic-size pool, a basketball court, and a flash of brilliant golden wings. Kimmie demanded, "What is *that?*"

"You wanna come meet my buddies? You got to play nice, you come out here. These are shy folks, mostly."

"But what kind of birds are they?"

"I got just about everything." He offered Kimmie a finger. "Cockatoos, parrots, songbirds from three continents."

She hesitated only a second. Amy held her daughter's forgotten blouse as she and Bob followed across the living room area and out to the aviary. The birds sang a gentle hello while Kimmie peered through the mesh. She listened as the giant named one bird after another. Finally, she asked, "Why are you so tall?"

"Because my momma told me I had to eat just two things—peanut butter and everything she put on my plate."

Kimmie still held the big man's finger. "I like peanut butter."

"Then you come to the right place, baby girl. You want some now?"

"I'm sleepy."

"I got rooms all fixed up for everybody, baby girl. Right this way."

But they were only partway across the living room when the night was punctuated by gunfire. Kareem surprised them all by pulling a pistol from his baggy shorts. "Don't y'all worry none. I done heard that drill before. Bob, you know how to use one of these?"

"I do."

"Take this one. Probably won't need it. We'll stay hunkered down. Trust the pros to do their job. The piece is for just in case."

Kimmie whimpered, "Scared, Mommy."

Kareem knelt and patted Kimmie's cheek. "Nobody's getting inside tonight, baby girl. You got the law and God on your side, you hear what I'm saying?"

Special Agent Ken Grant joined Granville and Paul in the car with Consuela. They drove down the street and parked out of sight of the house. Consuela directed the cops on sentry to do the same. The chief parked behind them and sat talking on her phone. They traded off doing patrols on foot. Granville and Paul and Consuela helped out. The chief stayed for another hour, then left without a word or a wave.

On the phone, Ken Grant briefed Tom Beeks between patrols, then cut the connection while there was still the sound of a complaining voice at the other end. Paul liked Ken a good deal at that moment. Enough to say, "You're doing the right thing, being allies with the local force on this."

Ken took his time responding. "Come tomorrow morning, Washington might think otherwise."

Granville tapped his wrist. "Actually, it's today."

Ken just sighed. "I liked it here. So did my family."

Consuela said, "We could always use another pro on the force."

Ken looked at her. Might have smiled. At least

his lips twitched. He was working on a response when Consuela's phone rang. Paul watched her come to full alert, going from sentry to warrior vixen, all in the space of two breaths. She did not bother to cup the phone as she reported, "We've got incoming."

"Where?"

"Our guys out front just spotted the two vehicles coming round for a second inspection of the front gates." Consuela listened, then added, "Both Escalades. One is missing the rear bumper."

Paul had his phone out. "The front gate is up, right?"

"And the security guard is on patrol at the development's far end," Consuela confirmed.

"Granville, let's move." Paul phoned Amy as he crossed the lawn. Bob opened the door for them. Paul watched Amy struggle to dress the whiny child and then he ushered them across the lawn. He did not draw his weapon until he was moving back into position.

Granville met him by the rear doors. "They've been joined by four more vehicles."

"Let me guess," Paul said. "Three new Vettes and a top-end Camaro."

"That's an affirm." Granville pulled a straight-backed chair up to the darkened front window. "Consuela asks, who gives us the green light?"

"Ask her how she feels about letting Ken Grant have the honor."

Granville passed on the query and grinned at the response. "The lady gives you a very spicy yes."

Paul stood by the window on the front door's opposite side. He disliked being inside the house. He wanted to be out where he could take the night's pulse. But he stayed where he was for the moment. Running through things. Using the last quiet moments as well as he possibly could.

Granville kept the phone to his left ear. His right hand was in his lap, holding a massive .38 Special. The gun glinted in the light through the window in front of him. He said, "The chief's been alerted and is on her way back. Two choppers have just left Sanford. Inbound in ten. Less. Ken Grant has pulled in his team, but they're coming from Orlando, so they'll probably miss the party. Shame."

Paul decided he had heard enough. "Tell the others I'll be stationed in the shrubs between us and the house next door. Ask them not to shoot me."

"Always better to take a hit from the bad guys," Granville agreed.

Paul had just settled into the shrubbery when the night shifted around him. The cicadas cut off their racket; even the frogs down by the lake went still. Then he heard it, the soft rumble of supercharged engines, growing until he could feel the sound in his chest. They angled to a halt in front of the house, one after the other, the two Escalades in the center. The engines were suddenly quiet. The occupants sat waiting.

Two men emerged from the Camaro and another pair from one of the Vettes. They cradled snub-nosed guns with both hands. Paul assumed the guns were Mossbergs, the automatic weapon of choice among lowlifes. The Mossberg was hard to aim, but that hardly mattered, since it could spray the twenty-eight bullets in its over-size clip so fast that they sounded like just one noise, a giant ripping of the fabric of life. The four men spread out, angled so they covered all the compass headings except what stood directly in front of the vehicles. The house was silent.

Then the night woke up.

It was as sweet a takedown as Paul had ever seen. The choppers arrived in a rush of sound and light, followed by six police cars careening through the front gates and Consuela and the sentry cops flashing the lights on their cars from the other way. All exits blocked, all resistance futile. The cars and their occupants were trapped in the amber of overpowering opposition. The bullhorn only punctuated what had already gone down.

"This is the police and the DEA! Come out with your hands empty! You are under arrest!"

— Chapter 34 —

The news that Bob Denton was stepping out with a woman he had hired to paint designs on his dealership's windows stayed secret for another seventy-two hours. But that was enough for their date to be overshadowed by the fireworks of a federal investigation. Denton Chevrolet became home to a team of forensic accountants and DEA agents, all of whom were intent upon ferreting out anyone with known associations to Bob Denton, Jr. Two members of Bob's sales staff were already in federal custody, as was Bob's son. Coming face-to-face with the very real prospect of a lengthy jail stint had erased BeeJay's smirk.

Bob's son was singing up a storm, according to Granville and Paul. The motives and actions were as Amy had suspected. A small fishing port on Florida's Atlantic coast had been pinpointed as an ideal conduit for cocaine smuggling and offered the Ohio gang their very own supply line. They had intended to cut out the Miami mobs and pocket all the profits themselves, using new cars purchased from Brentonville dealerships they would soon own. Bob Jr. was to have been their front man.

Amy remained extremely busy overseeing the

forensic accountants poring over the dealership's books. Not to mention those of the Subaru and Cadillac dealerships that Bob co-owned.

Rachel, the saleswoman with the autistic son, caught up with Amy on the fourth morning after the arrests. She followed Amy into the staff kitchen and asked, "You going out with Bob again tonight?"

"There are no secrets in this place, are there?"

"Not anymore. The DEA is seeing to that." The woman had a lovely smile, creased by her own hard times and spiced by goodwill. "Way to go, girl."

"I didn't come here looking for love, Rachel."

"You know what? I actually believe you. Which makes it sweeter still."

"Then the answer is yes, we're taking Kimmie to the movies."

"Kimmie's your little girl?"

"She is. And she loves Pixar. She wants one of those lamps for her desk, the one that stomps on the letter and then looks around. Kimmie asked Bob if he could get her one for Christmas."

"So the two are bonding. That's nice." Rachel slid the door shut. "We need to get our stories straight. In case anyone asks, you were slipped in here as part of the undercover team."

Amy was shocked. "That is a lie from start to finish, and you know it."

"I know it now." If anything, her smile

broadened. "Too late, though. I already let it slip."

"To whom?"

"Oh, everybody. They all know you two are an item. I wanted to stop the snide little comments about gold-digging before they had a chance to sink in. Cool, huh?" Rachel patted Amy's arm. "You're good for the man. I knew that the instant you set off with him for the rehab center. So does everybody else around here who really cares for Bob."

Amy was mulling that over when Paul tracked her back to her desk and asked, "Got a minute?"

"Not really." She pointed to the pair of forensic accountants who were arguing over an entry in her database. "I've got to keep an eye on those two, make sure they don't turn Bob's books into party hats."

Paul slid into the chair on the other side of her desk. "You can come back. It's safe."

"Back?"

"To your apartment. If you want. I've cleared it with the police. They agree."

"That's great." Amy heard the hollow note in her voice and wondered if Paul did, too. "What about you?"

"Lucy says I can keep the place as long as I need it."

"No. I mean—"

"I know what you mean." Paul angled his

body so his softly spoken words were pointed away from the accountants. "There's a church in Minneapolis. They need me."

"So go." But the words caught in her throat, such that she had to swallow hard before she could add, "What you do is important."

"Okay, sure. But I've been thinking, well . . ."

"You need us."

It was hard to say who was most surprised by her quiet declaration, Amy or Paul. He nodded slowly. "You're right. I do. This place is more than an assignment. I've made friends. I've found . . ."

"A place where you want to put down roots. I understand."

"You do, don't you?" He breathed deep. "Granville wants to team up. And Dan Eldridge. Go with me. Do this thing. Come back. Make it a regular sort of posting."

Amy felt her face draw into lines that were gradually becoming familiar. As though she had to trust tomorrow just to give in to the pleasure of a smile. "I know what Lucy would say."

"What is that?"

She reached over and gripped his hand. "Welcome home."

READING GROUP GUIDE AND AUTHOR Q&A

THE SIGN PAINTER
DAVIS BUNN

Amy Dowell had always considered herself a very good mother. But when she loses her husband to illness and her home to debt, she finds herself and her young daughter, Kimberly, living on the streets. She struggles to find a job that will get them back on their feet again.

When Amy meets Lucy Watts, the administrator of the church program that provides Amy and Kimberly with a meal, Lucy surprises Amy by setting them up in temporary housing. The same day, another church member offers Amy a job painting signs at his Chevrolet dealership. Still, Amy is afraid to let go and trust. Could this be the break she's been praying for? Can she afford to expose herself and Kimberly to the possibility of disappointment by hoping again?

QUESTIONS FOR DISCUSSION

1. Discuss the significance of the title, *The Sign Painter*. What are some of the signs that appear to Amy, Lucy, Bob, and Paul?

2. Both Amy and Lucy possess the skill of making quick assessments of other people and their intentions. Were Amy's first impressions of others always correct? Was Lucy right about Amy?

3. Amy has built up a fear and dislike of the police over her months on the road, but slowly comes to trust and befriend Paul Travers and Granville Burnes. How do you see Amy starting to trust again throughout the novel?

4. What do you make of Amy taking the money from the dealership? Do you think she did the right thing?

5. Why does Amy accept the job at Denton Chevrolet? Is this a good decision for her and Kimmie?

6. Consider the theme of friendship and support networks throughout the novel. How are the relationships between Amy and Lucy and Granville and Paul necessary and beneficial to each of the characters?

7. Which character do you identify with the most? Why?

8. Paul finally opens up and admits to feeling unfulfilled and bereft of purpose in his life. How does the theme of overcoming hard times through faith and sharing struggles with others appear throughout the novel?

9. How does Amy work to create a routine and a sense of home and normalcy for Kimmie? Does she succeed in teaching these things to her daughter? Consider this moment in the novel:

   When the service was over, Amy remained seated beside her little girl. It was a habit she had started soon after they hit the road. Amy wanted her daughter to hold on to all the good things that remained within reach. She could not tell such lessons to a child. She had to show them: Here was safety. Here was a place where she could feel connected to all the goodness in the world. This was a true sanctuary from life's uneven hand. And Kimmie needed to feel it for herself. (p. 96)

10. How does Amy use prayer as a tool in her life? How does it bring her closer to Lucy and Bob?

11. Compare the two parent-child relationships in *The Sign Painter*: Amy and Kimmie and Bob

Denton and Bob Jr. How does each relationship illustrate the challenges of being a parent?

12. What would you do if your neighborhood were facing drug-related violence like the church community in *The Sign Painter*?

13. The very last words of the novel are "Welcome home." How were the concepts of home, belonging, and community interwoven throughout the novel?

ENHANCE YOUR BOOK CLUB

1. Volunteer with your book group for an organization that helps homeless women and children. Visit http://www.nationalhomeless. org/directories/index.html to find your local, state, or national housing or homeless advocacy coalition, or make a financial contribution to support their work.

2. Check out Davis Bunn's other novels available from Howard Books: *Book of Dreams*, *Hidden in Dreams*, *The Black Madonna*, and *Gold of Kings*. Davis is known for writing excellent female and male protagonists. After reading one of his other books, compare and contrast your favorite characters from each book.

3. Find out more about the author by visiting www.DavisBunn.com. Discover more about Davis's upcoming projects, and discuss with other readers in the web forums. If you submit a review of *The Sign Painter*, it might be shared on Davis's blog!

A CONVERSATION WITH DAVIS BUNN

What was the inspiration behind *The Sign Painter*?

We have all seen homeless people on our streets—from small towns to large cities across America. Often we hurry past them, but later we reflect on the twists of fate that may have brought them so low—poverty, illness, mental problems, addictions, domestic violence. As Christians, in the spirit of Matthew 25:31–46, we may be moved to help "the least of these." For me, a turning point was when I saw a local news item in Florida. The recession had hit hard, unemployment was rife, and the housing boom had turned to bust. The report showed how entire families were being displaced, losing their homes and belongings to repossession orders. In desperation, many were reduced to living in vans or in rundown motels on the outskirts of Orlando's sprawl. I was moved by the plight of the children in particular—deprived of stability and security. Even their favorite pets and toys had to be abandoned. As I learned more about these problems and how Christian ministries tried to respond to them, I decided to write a story. But I did not want to focus on the hardships; I wanted to focus on the rebuilding. To my mind, too much attention is given to the falling down, and not enough to the getting back up again. So *The Sign Painter* aims toward hope and healing—a new future for homeless families, but also a reminder about the help our communities may be able to offer.

The *Sign Painter* covers some weighty problems of homelessness, unemployment, drug trafficking, and drug-related violence. Why did you choose to include these difficult issues?

Before addressing this question, let me first say that my primary aim here was to create an entertaining, encouraging novel. To say that the story is about these difficult problems really does not, at least as far as I am concerned, capture the true heart of this novel. *The Sign Painter* is a message of hope.

That said, the problem of homelessness does not exist by itself—it is part of a larger situation that our cities and our communities face. What I wanted to show was how certain churches have become involved in reclaiming their communities. There are some real heroes in this struggle, and they operate on the same principle as Jesus: One lost soul at a time.

The special operations and police maneuvers executed by Paul and Granville were so fun to read and so expertly detailed. Did you do any special research for those scenes?

This was a very special component of preparing to write *The Sign Painter*. Two friends on the local police force in Florida helped enormously in creating realistic characters. The character of Paul is actually a retired federal officer, and his portrait was based on friends who work in Washington.

As I was sketching these preliminary scenes, I had a dear friend whose church went through a very difficult period of upheaval. Over lunch with several pastor friends, they mentioned how sometimes what really was needed was a private investigator who was first and foremost a believer and who would work with the church toward restoration and healing. That was how the idea for Paul began—a roving former federal agent, dedicated to helping churches through threatening times.

How does your approach to writing a stand-alone novel differ from that for the series novels that you've written?

Well, in some cases, I feel like one novel contains pretty much everything I want to say on a subject. In others, I am kind of glad to walk away from the characters involved. But since completing *The Sign Painter*, I find myself working through scenarios where Paul and his new Florida team help other churches. So who knows? There may actually be another episode, in the fullness of time.

Which of the characters in *The Sign Painter* was the most fun to write? Which character was the most difficult?

Bob Denton became a real surprise for me. Initially I thought he would be a sort of "walk-on" part, someone who just serves as Amy's boss, and when the drug issue arises he then becomes a red herring—a person under suspicion who turns out to be a good guy in the end. But when I actually started writing, this man just took on a life of his own. He completely refused to do what I expected of him. Characters can be very bullheaded at times. Bob was determined to fall in love with Amy. I can't describe it any better than that.

It was heartbreaking to read about the broken relationship between Bob Denton and Bob Jr. What did you want readers to take away from their relationship?

This was very personal, and quite rough to write. There are people I'm very close to who have fallen into the trap of addiction. Enduring their trials and struggles has been tough. But the experiences have also opened my eyes to how a person needs help to break free. And some people, alas, do not either seek or wish to do so. For the story to work, I needed a Bob Jr. to represent those people who are content to dwell in the dark.

The themes of community and belonging are very prevalent in this book. How have these concepts been important in your own life?

I left home at age twenty and traveled to Europe for graduate studies. I basically never returned. After graduating I taught university for a year, then worked for an Arab consortium for three years, then became a consultant living in Germany. It was here, in Dusseldorf, that I came to faith.

For my entire adult life, community has never been easy, or readily available. This is one of the hardest aspects of living overseas. I have made homes in seven different countries, and each time it has been necessary to rebuild my community—

new friends, new church, new sense of belonging. In some cases this was very difficult. When I began work on this story, I found myself hearing repeatedly from the former homeless what it meant to rebuild their personal communities. How hard it was to trust, to hope, and what a vital role the church played in helping them heal. It was at this level that I most identified with them—how crucial it was to find a church that truly lived the concept of open doors and open arms.

What are you working on next?

I stay very busy crafting new stories in a variety of genres. This period of my life has become especially intense, as I have also become involved in teaching creative writing at the university level, and I am engaged in several multimedia projects, including film production and radio broadcasting.